The Amish Nurse Series #2

Time Will Tell

Stephanie Schwartz

Glossary

Ach!—Plain expression meaning "Oh!"

Amische—Pennsylvania Dutch dialect word meaning "The Amish."

Ankela—Hutterish word for "grandmother."

Ausbund—German hymn book used by Plain churches.

Basel—Hutterish word meaning "woman."

Bickel—Pennsylvania Dutch dialect word meaning "pickle."

Bobbel—Pennsylvania Dutch dialect word meaning "baby" singular.

Bobbeli—Pennsylvania Dutch dialect word meaning "babies" plural.

Boolah—Hutterish word meaning "little man."

Clöps—Hutterish word meaning "hamburger."

Dat—Pennsylvania Dutch dialect word referring to or addressing one's father.

Dawdi haus—Pennsylvania Dutch dialect word meaning "a grandparents' apartment usually attached to a main house."

Denke—Pennsylvania Dutch dialect word meaning "thank you."

Dindla—Hutterish word meaning "little girl," affectionate.

Ditchly—Pennsylvania Dutch dialect word meaning "head scarf/bandana" used for work/chores.

Doddy—Pennsylvania Dutch dialect word meaning or when addressing one's "Grandfather."

Englische(rs)—Pennsylvania Dutch dialect general term meaning "non-Amish" (-ers plural.)

Ferhoodled—Pennsylvania Dutch dialect word meaning "mixed up, flummoxed, crazy."

Fespa—German word for "afternoon snack."

Formavorscht—German word for "fresh sausage."

Frischi Wascht—Pennsylvania Dutch dialect word meaning a "sausage and noodle dish."

Frolic—Pennsylvania Dutch term for a "scheduled gathering with a single purpose in mind."

Geiste—Pennsylvania Dutch dialect word meaning "Ghost" or "Spirit."

Glums koki—German word for "cottage cheese cakes."

Gott—Pennsylvania Dutch dialect word meaning "God."

Gut—Pennsylvania Dutch dialect word meaning "good."

Guten nacht—German phrase meaning "Good night."

Grossmammi—Pennsylvania Dutch dialect word meaning or addressing one's "Grandmother."

Haus—Pennsylvania Dutch dialect word meaning "house."

Hinkelhaus—Pennsylvania Dutch dialect word meaning "chicken house."

'Hof—Hutterish word shortened from Bruderhof meaning the 'Place of the Brothers.'

Hutterische—The language and people called Hutterites.

Kapp—Pennsylvania Dutch dialect word meaning "prayer cap/bonnet."

Kesslehaus—Pennsylvania Dutch dialect word meaning "wash house."

Kinner—Pennsylvania Dutch dialect word meaning "children" (plural.)

Klanaschuel—Hutterish dialect word meaning "baby house or baby school/nursery."

Kopftuch—Hutterish dialect word meaning "traditional head covering or scarf."

Kuchen—German word meaning "cake, cobbler, a sweet dessert."

Kumm—Pennsylvania Dutch dialect word meaning "come."

Mamm—Pennsylvania Dutch dialect word to address one's "mother; mom."

Mammi—Pennsylvania Dutch dialect word meaning "Grandma" (familiar.)

Maud—Pennsylvania Dutch dialect word meaning "maid" usually hired.

Mudder—Hutterish dialect word meaning "Mother."

Mufti—German slang word meaning "mischief."

Ol' vetter—Hutterish dialect word meaning "Grandpa."

Onkel—Pennsylvania Dutch dialect word meaning "Uncle."

Ordnung—Plain word used by both Hutterites, Amish and Mennonites meaning "the written and unwritten rules and traditions of the Plain communities."

Paska—German word for traditional "Easter sweet bread."

Patties—'Patties down,' Pennsylvania Dutch dialect word meaning "hands down" as in prayer, instructing children.

Pennsylfaanisch Deitsch—The Pennsylvania Dutch dialect.

Pierogi—a German filled dumpling.

Rivvels—Pennsylvania Dutch dialect word meaning a "tiny dumpling," usually made with noodle dough rubbed through a grater and dropped into boiling water or broth.

Roasht—Pennsylvania Dutch dialect word meaning "a stuffing mixture often served with chunks of chicken or turkey, baked and accompanied by gravy."

Rumschpringe—A rite of passage for Amish youth in their teens; a time to explore their options outside of their communities before making a life commitment to the church.

Samschdaag—Pennsylvania Dutch dialect word meaning "Saturday."

Schachdel—Pennsylvania Dutch dialect word meaning "old woman."

Schmunzling—Pennsylvania Dutch dialect word meaning "hugging and kissing."

Schweschder—Pennsylvania Dutch dialect word meaning "sister."

Sits ana—Pennsylvania Dutch dialect word meaning "(please) sit down."

Schnitz—Pennsylvania Dutch dialect word meaning "dried apple."

Schtruvvels—Pennsylvania Dutch dialect word meaning "stray hairs."

Shem—Pennsylvania Dutch dialect word meaning "shame."

Shlaf gut—German phrase meaning "sleep well."

Shunned—Pennsylvania Dutch word meaning a church action or discipline for serious sin. Repentance needs to be demonstrated before the member can return to the community.

Strankel—Hutterish dialect word meaning "ham, potato and green bean soup."

Tract—Plain word found in Pennsylvania Dutch and Hutterish meaning "religious clothing."

Vereniki—a "German dumpling."

Vetter—Hutterish dialect word meaning "man/men."

Weschkich—Pennsylvania Dutch dialect word meaning "washroom."

Wunderbar-gut—Pennsylvania Dutch dialect word meaning "wonderful and good."

Ya—Pennsylvania Dutch dialect word meaning "yes."

Youngie—Pennsylvania Dutch dialect word meaning "the youth."

Ztzvilling—Pennsylvania Dutch dialect word meaning "twins."

Zwieback—Hutterish dialect word meaning "bread buns" in this case "hamburger buns."

Recap

Phoebe Schwartz had tried her best to remain faithful while resigned to living a single life within her Amish community, surrounded by friends and family, many of whom have large families and seemingly endless babies. She had accepted that this was all part of God's plan for her, at least until Fate or Divine Wisdom deemed otherwise. Her friends at the nursing program, Susanna, Leah and Hilda—also members of the Plain churches in the area—are seeking to live holy lives too, 'while in the world, but not of it.'

Phoebe's life changes forever when the district's Amish bishops ask the seemingly impossible of her. Never in a thousand years could she have imagined this would be required of her. Does she have the faith to follow through on their request? Could she ever have imagined the blessings this *fiat*, this Yes to God's will brings with it?

Part One

Chapter One

Finally, everyone was tucked in, flashlights by their beds ready should anyone need to get up during the night to head to the outhouse. Phoebe bid them all a *guten nacht* before returning downstairs to join Stephen in the *dawdi haus,* the little addition on the main house built for the grandparents. They would live there until she finished school and then swap places with her parents who were still in the larger main farmhouse. Hilde was in the narrow cot and Susanna and Leah shared the double bed in the upstairs room.

"This is amazing, really," Hilde began as they all waited for sleep to take them. "I didn't really have any idea."

"Me either," Leah added. "It's like going back to olden times."

"But they aren't old fashioned," Susanna pondered. "Do you know what I mean? Not simple or uneducated. They're where the rest of the twenty-first Century is in some ways, but the culture is back in the first part of last century in everything else. They educate themselves and they are aware of the rest of the world in many ways, keeping up, but choosing not to follow the trends, the styles."

"Or all the inventions and progress. So, it makes for a very interesting interpretation of Plain. By choosing which ways to modernize as a group, they've retained a whole way of life. It is fascinating," Leah concluded.

"But," Hilde began, "we've chosen not to have TVs or computers or radios at home and live together, sharing everything —values, church—but the Mennonites have chosen to modernize and we can still live a Plain lifestyle."

Susanna agreed, "And as Hutterites, we have too—modernized —to keep up with the farming and all. It makes it easier to compete in the market, but the Amish have sort of shot themselves in the foot there. That's why they are so much poorer, economically at least, than we are. They can't compete when Big Ag is taking over, so they have to think up other ways, but then loads of them end up catering to tourism and such, which is a pretty poor trade off if they want to be left alone to practice what they believe, if you ask me. It must be a constant struggle. It's gotta be."

"But it makes for good romance novels, huh?" Leah added. "Even with the tourists, they've kept their home life private, and that's made for all the mystery about them. It isn't all rosy, for sure. Well, *we* know that now, but everyone who buys the romance books doesn't and they think it is all just dating and getting married, baking and eating pies and having babies. And then the Amish don't get a penny off the publishing business. I read, don't you know, that some of those authors have sold over thirty-four *million* books so far? That's almost criminal. And that each year half of all the paperbacks sold in this country are romance, and Amish romance books are in there too."

Susanna said, "Do you know what I once read? The publishing business calls them 'bonnet books,' because they say, 'just put a bonnet on the cover and it will sell.' I wonder if I wrote one of those books and put my *Hutterische kopftuch* on it if it would sell. Maybe we are in the wrong profession, ladies."

"Well, good night. I'm done in," Hilde spoke from the cot. "Do we get to sleep in?"

"Yeah," Leah answered. "Good night," she whispered.

Then, as an afterthought, Hilde asked, "Will Phoebe get us up to help milk the cows?"

"Good night, Hilde!" Leah repeated.

Phoebe didn't sleep in but got up when she heard *Mamm* rummaging around in the kitchen on the other side of the *dawdi haus* door. She would be starting breakfast for when *Dat* and Stephen came in from chores and the girls all came down from upstairs. Phoebe wanted to help.

She had returned to school after the horrible tornado that had decimated the old college. All the students had been absorbed into other colleges throughout the state. The three other Plain girls in her LPN program, who together called themselves The Four Musketeers, had become best friends during their first year together. They had been invited to visit Susanna's Hutterite colony last month, which had come as quite a revelation to Phoebe who is Amish and Hilde and Leah who are Mennonite. It was Phoebe's turn to host the others, and she couldn't be more excited.

"Morning, *Mamm*," Phoebe greeted her. "What can I do?"

"Well, for one, go out to the chickens and get all the eggs there. Should be enough for everyone. Oh, and get me some big leaves of basil for the top of the breakfast pizza. *Denke.*"

Phoebe slipped on her mud boots in the entry room off the kitchen, picked up the basket on the shelf there and headed out to the chickens. They were all pecking about the ground out in the yard, so it was a good time to catch them off their nests. They were free-range chickens, which they could then advertise at the farm stand, charging buyers accordingly. She went into the dark little hen hut, feeling into each box for eggs. She was taken aback when she found a chicken in one of the boxes. She must have surprised the hen too, who lunged out and pecked at her, warning her off the precious eggs she was guarding. *Mamm* hadn't told her there was a broody one this late in the fall, but the hen definitely had sitting in mind and staying put and defending it no matter what.

"Well, then. Don't worry, henny. You can keep your eggs. Just don't peck me," she cooed to the chicken. *I wonder if* mamms *get broody when they're expecting,* Phoebe thought to herself. *I've heard about 'nesting' toward the end of nine months, getting everything ready. I doubt chickens get morning sickness, though* she chuckled as the thought occurred to her. *And basil,* she reminded herself as she went to open the kitchen door. Spinning around, she went back out toward the garden and plucked a handful of the shiny leaves, sniffing the spicy goodness on her way back.

She came in, kicking off her boots at the door and brought in the eggs, setting them by the sink.

"*Mamm,* did you know the Sussex chicken is broody? She pecked me when I went to check for eggs."

"Oh, yes. I forgot to tell you. She'll have some fine chicks," *Mamm* answered. "Nine eggs, I think."

Phoebe washed her hands and started setting the table. "We're going to the singing tonight. I think that will be *gut* fun for them. Don't you? So don't make us supper tonight. We'll eat there."

"Quiet, I am reading this recipe. I haven't made breakfast pizza for a while," *Mamm* said as she ran her finger along the list of ingredients on the recipe she had cut out of *The Budget* newspaper, the 'Cookin' With Maudie' column in particular. *The Budget* is a Plain newspaper serving the Amish and Mennonites throughout North and South America and Canada. A scribe in each colony or settlement contributes a weekly recap of any news in his or her community. Without the use of computers or phones, it has become a very sought-after means of keeping up with others near and far.

"The dough is over there if you want to roll it out. Use the biggest square pan with grease and then sprinkle it with corn meal and garlic salt, would *ya?*"

Phoebe rolled out the pizza crust and then quietly set the table before putting on a fresh pot of coffee.

"I was going to make a batch of pumpkin whoopie pies this afternoon. Want to take some to the singing? *Mamm* asked.

"No, Emily said they are all set for snacks. You'll need them for when the boys come with their families for dinner tomorrow noon," Phoebe reminded her.

"Yes, true," *Mamm* agreed, continuing to nod her head as she resumed reading the recipe.

"No church tomorrow, so we can help with dinner before we take off visiting in the morning," Phoebe said.

"Just don't be late for Sunday dinner," *Mamm* scolded. "And come with an appetite, *ya?* Don't fill up on snacks all morning."

"What are you making for it?" Phoebe asked.

"Well, Abe's are bringing all the pies—Fiona is making her famous lemon meringue, and Isaac's Hannah Mary is bringing bread and a corn pone," *Mamm* told her. She continued, "I'm going to make the chicken and dumplings from the last of last year's canned in the root cellar, and then pickled beets, fried sweet potatoes, and coleslaw."

"Don't outdo yourself, *Mamm,*" Phoebe reminded her. "We don't want you all worn out when they come. Let us help in the morning, *ya?*"

"*Ya,* okay. I was going to do the potatoes and the coleslaw ahead, today. Should be *gut* fun to see them all."

"I've been so busy with school I haven't really been with their *kinner* for ages. At least I see them at church every other Sunday, otherwise I'd never see them at all and they wouldn't know me. I can't wait till I'm done with college. It seems like that's all I've done for my whole life," Phoebe reflected.

"But you're getting toward the end, and already helping folks around here, too," *Mamm* added. "That was sure a mind wave when the bishops asked you to become a nurse. It had never been done before but turned out to be really brilliant, eh?"

"I think you mean 'brain wave,' *Mamm.*"

"It's the same thing, and you know that. Don't always go correcting me now that you are educated. Do you do that to Stephen, too? I hope not. It is intimidating," *Mamm* scowled at her before turning back to the recipe, adding, "and that's no way to keep a husband!"

Phoebe changed the subject. "Did you know that Annie Gingerich is actually telling people they can *kumm* to their place on Mondays after school if they want me to tell them what to do about their ailments and find out what I think? She has a whole list of names of who I should see. Can you believe it? She's keeping the kitchen clear on Mondays, too, so I can visit with them in there. She's setting up a whole clinic, for goodness' sake. Telling who can see me next, keeping the others on the porch or in the living room till it's their turn. Can you imagine? All I can do is tell them what I know and tell them to see a doctor. Don't they already know that *Mamm?*" Phoebe pleaded.

"No, they don't. We've only had that evil man, Dr. Adams, all these years. He has built up his own little kingdom, that hospital, on Plain people's money. We don't trust a word out of his mouth anymore," *Mamm* said.

"I know. I told my teacher about him, that he seems to be doing C-sections for all the *mamms* who come in to have their ninth or tenth *bobbeli,* which gets him ten times more money; that he's even sterilizing Plain women without their knowledge or consent when they go in to have *bobbeli,* thinking he is *Gott* and deciding to take the so-called 'population problem' into his own hands. He just tells the *dats* that their wife started bleeding and he had to do an emergency C-section and saved her just in time, but she can't have any more kids, but then they thank him! *They thank him!* Thinking he saved their wives. She promised to look into it and get to the proper authorities to help us. I can hardly believe what's he's done. Right under our noses. How does he think he can get away with that?"

"He thinks we're all stupid cows. That we don't know any better, that's what I think," *Mamm* answered, shaking her head.

"I think our cows are probably smarter than he is, too."

The girls came down the stairs at that point.

"Mmmm. Something smells wonderful!" Susanna explained. "Can we help?"

"No, all done," *Mamm* said, smiling as she picked up her mug of coffee from the counter and settled in her chair at the table.

"Let me do the serving at least," Phoebe begged.

"Fine with me," *Mamm* answered, sipping her cold coffee. "Is that new pot ready yet?"

Chapter Two

The first stop that morning on Phoebe's tour of the Amish settlement for her three school mates was at the little one-room schoolhouse. The ride in the buggy was quite a novelty for the other girls. Leah and Hilde were from Mennonite churches and had also been asked to go to college to get their LPN license by their communities. Susanna was from a Hutterite colony that had hit upon the same idea, to send an older girl to get a nurse's training in order to help their people both at home with their sick and elderly members and at the neighboring hospitals when they needed to go in.

"So, this is how you get around summer and winter, too?" Leah asked incredulously, as Alice slowly clip-clopped up to the hitching rail.

"Ya, this is it," Phoebe said. "Unless we're going to a wedding far away or a special doctor trip or something. Then we hire one of the drivers from our area. You know, you don't rush out to the store whenever you need one or two things only. We plan the trips to town or wherever. Each district is measured off by the farthest buggy ride to church meetings. Forty-five minutes is about tops. If the district grows out from that, they start a new one."

"I bet it is less stressful without driving all over and rushing around?" Hilde asked.

"I think stress is also what you make it. If you bite off more than you can chew, taking on a project or whatever, you can get pretty stressed out doing that, too. I don't think it's limited to driving," Phoebe pondered.

"I think you are right. If I put off my homework till Sunday night on the weekend, I can get pretty stressed out too," Susanna observed. "Then I stay up too late, have to get up early, drink too much coffee and it ruins the whole day."

"But I like the pace of things around here," Leah noted. "I just like it. It feels less hurried, I guess."

They went into the school to find Teacher Esther sitting at the queen-size quilting frame with some of her students.

"*Ach,* what a *wunderbar* quilt!" Phoebe exclaimed. "It's a double wedding band. Is it for your wedding?"

"Yes," Esther replied. "I like this pattern, too, I think as much as the one we made for your wedding. Do you ladies want to help us for a bit?"

"Oh, yes," Susanna said, pulling up a chair. "We make quilts, but they're all machine quilted now. Only last year we got a long arm computerized quilting machine. Other colonies come to us to use it all the time. It's quite amazing. Before that we used a regular Pfaff sewing machine with all the attachments to quilt with. It wasn't easy, it could get so bunched up. You couldn't spread it out as well. So how do I quilt this?"

"First, you put one hand under the quilt, and then hold the needle in your right hand, if you're righthanded," Esther explained. "Then you sew little stitches in a line, two or three running stitches at a time between the safety pins holding it all in place on each side of the chalk lines. They don't have to be super tiny. I like to do about five stitches to an inch since I have a thick batting inside this one. The quilts at the state fair are super thin, and they often manage up to twelve stitches per inch, that is six on top and six underneath. Your hand underneath should just feel the tip of the needle to be sure it's gone all the way through before going back up. That's it. Yours looks perfect."

They all sat down and sewed for about an hour, visiting the whole time.

Susanna's needle ran out of thread. Esther showed her how to tie it off and hide the knot by going back into the last hole with the needle and popping the knot into the inside of the quilt, cutting off the extra thread left on the outside. Then she said she wanted to show them how to thread a needle properly.

"First, I have to tell you a little story that I tell all of my students." They all stopped sewing and looked up.

She continued. "There was once a prince and his parents said it was high time he found a wife. His parents put out a call to the whole kingdom for marriageable girls to come to the castle for a ball so he could find a wife. Of course, he was completely overwhelmed by the sheer numbers of all the girls who would like to marry him and showed up. So, he decided to hold a competition. All of them would have to sew a blanket and the first one done would become his wife. So, they all sat down and the servants brought them everything they'd need: fabric, scissors, needles and thread and they began. Quickly, the girls pulled long threads off the spools and threaded the needles and began. But there was one wise girl who cut off short threads, like this," Esther demonstrated with a thread only about twelve inches long. "The others thought to themselves, 'surely it will take her forever at that rate,' but the fact of the matter was that the other girls that had pulled off long threads kept getting tangled up and got knots and had to keep starting over while the wise girl just forged on ahead with her short threads. Of course she got to be his wife. And they really loved each other, too--just so you know." They all laughed at that.

"I think I will always remember that now when I am sewing," Susanna said. "You're going to the singing tonight, aren't you?" Esther asked the others.

Phoebe answered first. "We wouldn't miss it for the world."

"I can't wait," Susanna said. "I just wish Levi could be here. He's my fiancé. We're getting married in November."

"So are we," Esther exclaimed. "I can hardly wait."

"Well, dearies. We have another stop to make," Phoebe reminded them. "I want to check in at the Gingerich's before it gets too much later. I told you about them, the *dat* that wanted so badly to get out of the hospital and he's at home now. He's been home two weeks already. He's pretty close to Eternity, but so peaceful. His wife Annie is an angel. It's always special to be there with them. I love it when I get to be there when they sing to him at night. He smiled yesterday when they were singing. The children are so dear. His grandchildren hold his hands and sing, too. They like the hymns, especially about the angels and about heaven."

The Gingerich's farm was only about fifteen minutes away by buggy.

"Makes me want to start a quilt," Susanna said as they drove along. "'Can't wait till school's done, though."

They pulled the buggy up to the house and quietly went in. Annie met them in the kitchen.

"These are my pals from the nursing program, Annie: Hilde, Leah, and Susanna. We wanted to see how he is this afternoon," Phoebe said.

"My, my. We could open our own hospital with all these nurses," Annie chuckled. "He's quiet. Not sipping much, but no fever. I have plenty of help tonight so I can rest and someone will get me up if I'm needed."

"That's *gut*. May we go in?" Phoebe asked.

"Yes, yes, for sure. But if he can't swallow now and can't take the pills, should I give him the morphine like you showed me?" Annie asked.

"Only if he appears in pain or agitated at all. The doctor said we could give it every three hours. Do you want me to stop by after the singing tonight just to check in with you? It's no trouble at all," she offered.

"Yes, that would be *wunderbar*. I can watch how you do it then. Just to be sure. I still have those prefilled injections you gave me in the 'fridge," Annie added.

"*Gut.* See you later, then," Phoebe concluded.

The next stop was at Phoebe's grandmother's *dawdi haus* next to Barbara's farm. *Grossmammi* met them at the door. "*Kumm* in, *kumm* in," she motioned. "Is this ever a treat. Look at you, will *ya*. You're all nurses, eh? My, are we in *gut* hands, then. I just put the coffee pot on. Will *ya* have some?" As *Mammi* puttered, she continued,

"I sure wasn't in agreement with the bishops when they decided to send you to college, Phoebe. No sir! Most *ferhoodled* thing I'd ever heard of. Had they lost their minds I said to myself. Sending young girls out into the world with all sorts. They weren't gonna ruin you if I had anything to say about it, exposing you to everything worldly out there. And I let them know what I thought, too. Boy, did they get an earful, I tell *ya*. Sure did. But they didn't budge. Now I am actually glad you went. I can't believe I said that. Well, now you're helping our sick ones, helping *mamms* and all."

"Yes, coffee, *denke,*" Phoebe said as she hugged her beloved grandma. "*Mamm* sent some of her whoopie pies for you. There are chocolate, oatmeal and pumpkin ones. She's making more today, but these were in the kerosene freezer and she wants us to use them up. Let me introduce you to everyone," she began.

"Are you enjoying your visit?" *Mammi* asked the others.

"Very much," Susanna said. "It is so different from how I grew up in the colony. Some things are the same, but then others are all new to me. I'm so glad we could come."

Leah spoke next. "Any books I read that I thought were really what your life is like weren't true at all. The Amish aren't as old-fashioned as the books make you think. It's so much more like what we live for, though it is definitely still miles away from the English. I suppose the outside world thinks Mennonites are living in the Dark Age, too, or at least the Middle Ages."

"And everyone's been so friendly. I hope we can visit again. We've become so close to Phoebe, I hope our friendship lasts forever," Hilde added.

"I do too," *Mammi* answered. "I hear you've been looking in on Annie and Gary. How is he?"

Phoebe explained, "He's very close to Eternity but so peaceful. I'm glad. We'll see them again tonight after the *youngie* singing."

"'Be life long or short, its completeness depends on what it was lived for,'" *Mammi* recited from one of her proverbs. "The Gingerichs are such a faithful family. *Denke* for helping them."

"No, it's an honor for me," Phoebe said.

"This is good coffee. What kind is it?" Hilde asked.

"Oh, it's decapitated. The doctor said that's the only kind I can drink now. It's not too bad," *Mammi* replied.

"Ah... *Mammi*... do you mean it's de-CAFF-in-a-ted?" Phoebe carefully enunciated.

"That's what I said." *Mammi* frowned at her. The girls all looked down into their mugs, stifling giggles that threatened to erupt, not wanting to offend Phoebe's grandmother.

Pheebs let this one go, she said to herself. *Well, now I know where my* mamm *gets it from, I guess.*

They visited for close to an hour and then bid *Mammi* goodbye, each girl hugging her and thanking for the visit.

"Be sure and see me next time you *kumm*, okay?" she made them promise.

The Four Musketeers still had Barbara to visit, so they walked around to the back of the big house and found the family in the yard. Barbara was hanging laundry on the lines with her baby next to her, secured in a highchair with an odd assortment of toys tied by shoelaces to one of the spindles on the side of the chair. The other children came running when they saw they had visitors, but then, not recognizing them, except for Phoebe who looked somewhat familiar, they tried to hide behind their mother's very ample, bright rose-colored skirt which was billowing in the wind.

"Hey, *yous,* come out. You remember your Auntie Phoebe. She married *Onkel* Stephen, *ya?*" Barbara tried to coax them out. "You were at that wedding not so long ago. Remember? Harold stepped on a nail near the barn when you were all running around at *Mammi's,* and we had to take him to the doctor afterwards."

Phoebe introduced the others to Barbara. The *kinner* slowly peeked out from behind their *mamm,* wondering who these strange ladies were. They didn't look *Englische,* yet they weren't *Amische* either. Two wore long dresses like their *mamm* but the fabric was flowered, definitely not *Amische,* but then they did wear white *kapps* similar to their *mamm's.* And then the other one was dressed almost showy, fancy it seemed to them: Plaid skirt and vest over a white puffy-sleeved blouse and a polka dotted kerchief to top it all off. Very strange, they surmised.

Phoebe bent down and peeked back at the little ones. "Hiya. *Kumm* see what your *Mammi* sent with me for you." That did the trick. "But you have to save your whoopie pies for after lunch, okay?" They all came out and solemnly nodded as each received his or her Saran-wrapped whoopie pie.

"Why are they called 'whoopie pies,' *Mamm?*" Harold wanted to know.

"Well, I heard tell that when some children found them in their lunch pails long ago, they shouted, 'whoopie' and they got to be called that," she explained. At that Harold shouted, "whoopie!" and threw his cookie into the air. He watched as it fell to the ground, smashing what had been a perfectly formed soft cookie sandwich only a few minutes ago. Good thing it was still wrapped up. He picked it up and examined it quietly for a few minutes.

Then Barbara lifted the baby out of the highchair, handing her to Phoebe. "I've got lunch all ready. I'll be right back," she called as she headed for the kitchen.

Phoebe turned toward the Musketeers and introduced the baby. "This is Merri. It's actually Merri Christmas. She was born last Christmas day."

"Oh, that is so cute!" Susanna laughed, taking the baby's hand in hers.

"She's about ten months?" Leah asked, tickling the little bare foot that stuck out by her.

"Almost. And now these are the boys: The oldest is Matthew, there, and then Mark, Luke and Harold," Phoebe pointed out in order of age. "Matthew and Mark started school when I was still teaching. You are so grown up now, eh?"

"I'll see if I can help carry anything," Hilde offered, heading toward the house.

"Maybe we should all sit down at the picnic table and we'll be ready when your *mamm kumms,*" Phoebe suggested. "Mark, would you get the highchair over here for me?"

Barbara and Hilde came out of the kitchen carrying lunch. "Here, take this tablecloth from me," Barbara asked as she turned toward Phoebe, who grabbed the checkered tablecloth out from under Barbara's arm.

The children were all quiet, their hands folded in their laps under the table, waiting patiently. Finally, Barbara sat down, bowed her head for a moment and then looked up. The children were still warily checking out the visitors. That is, until Harold spied the plate of cookies in the middle of the table and screamed, "Monster cookies! Yay!" while eyeing the huge cookies with M&Ms poking out from the dough.

"You could say 'whoopie' too," Matthew pointed out.

"But after your sandwich, Mister," Barbara warned him. Everyone laughed at that and enjoyed their lunch.

"These are sandwiches are great, but I can't quite put my finger on it. What's in them?" Susanna asked.

"Tongue," Barbara barely whispered.

"You've got to be kidding me," Hilde said. "My mom could never get us to eat tongue."

"We like it," Matthew said. "I like turning the crank on the grinder when *Mamm* makes it," he explained.

Luke chimed in at that with his mouth full. "I got to help, too."

Mark added, finally warming up to the company, "I got to put the pickle and the apple in the grinder. If you hurry and sit under the table and open your mouth, you get the apple juice on your tongue while its's cranking. Is that why it's called tongue, *Mamm?* 'Cause you catch the drips on your tongue? Huh?" Barbara agreed, "Uh huh," nodding her head in agreement and smiling slyly.

"I've got four brothers too," Leah told the children. "The oldest one is Nathan, then me, then Yosef, Yacob and Simon. Simon's about your age, Harold."

Susanna and Hilde also named their sibling. Hilde began. "We have three girls. I come first, then Anke, and then Greta, who is still a baby like your Merri."

Susanna then proceeded to tell the children about her large family. "We are eleven kids, and I come right in the middle." The children stopped chewing, and all looked up at *Mamm* at that, their eyes asking, 'how can that be possible?'

"Will we have eleven, *Mamm?*" Luke wanted to know.

Her diplomatic response was, "We'll see what the Lord sends, *ya?*" which didn't quite answer the question, but gave the firm impression that the answer would remain a vague one, and that the subject was closed. Luke was left quietly puzzling that one where he sat.

Susanna continued counting the names off on her fingers. "So, there's Patch, Winky, Boolah, *Kleiner Mann*—which means 'little man' 'cause he's so short—and Kitty who are all married. There are just too many Sams and Berthas and Rebeccas and Davids in all the colonies, so for a while we'd say Sam's Becky, and that got shortened to Sam-Becky, and then somewhere in there the nicknames just stuck. I come next and then after me are the youngest five: Henrietta, Pauline, Ian, Kemp and Tessa, who is two."

"Holy cow!" Luke exclaimed.

"Luke, you know that's forbidden," Barbara scolded. "Now hush. No more talking from you. Got it?"

Luke nodded, his face blushing at being reprimanded in front of company. He looked down at his bare feet as he nervously swung them under the table and remained silent for the rest of the meal.

"Do I have a nickname?" Harold asked finally.

"No, my sweet," Barbara answered. "Your name is just fine."

"Yeah," he replied. "Just like the Lord's."

"What?" Phoebe asked, the others at the table equally mystified.

"At church we always say, 'Harold be thy name.'" he answered plainly, completely clueless why his mother appeared so shocked.

"Oh, dear!" Barbara said, clearly stunned. When she could finally speak again she took a deep breath and began, "We actually say, 'hallowed,' which means 'holy.' HALL-owed be Thy name. It's not HAR-old. You were named after your *doddy,* who had just died when you were born." Harold didn't say anything, being left to ponder that one, too.

Susanna leaned over toward Phoebe on her right and whispered, "Like when my little sister thought we thank God for our jelly bread." Phoebe thought a minute until she got it. *Give us this day our daily bread,* she repeated to herself.

They had a delightful time visiting, until it was time to go. The children hung onto Phoebe, begging her to stay just a little while longer. They let her go finally when they got a promise from her to visit more often.

Chapter Three

After touring the surrounding district in the buggy, The Four Musketeers were finally destined for the singing being held at the Lapp's farm that weekend. After they picked up Stephen at his furniture workshop, they were on their way.

"I'm sure this will be the highlight of our visit," Susanna began.

"I'm excited," Leah said.

"Do you often have visitors at the singings?" Hilde wanted to know.

"Well, lots of families have relations visiting them throughout the year and the young people who are visiting with their families get invited, so they are new to the rest of us, but I don't remember any time other Plain boys or girls have ever come," Phoebe thought. "I have seen one or two *Amische youngie* who had left and come back."

"How can you tell, then?" Susanna asked.

Stephen had been listening quietly the whole time and decided to answer this one. "Well, we might have heard they'd written and asked to come back for a visit, or their hair is cut short or they're still wearing jeans, which usually means they're still undecided, but they are all welcome and no one tries to convince them they have to stay. They have to decide that for themselves. If this is how they grew up, they'll have to decide. For some, it's a no-brainer. They've seen the outside long enough to see how shallow it can be, and they want to live for something 'worth dying for' as *Mammi* says."

"It's no different for us," Susanna said. "Some leave us too, thinking the grass is greener somewhere else, that they won't have rules to follow, but most grow up pretty quick and decide. My *dat* always says 'a great deal depends on what we are looking for.' I often wonder why some are perfectly satisfied, grateful even, while others make themselves miserable, hankering for all else. It's a mystery," she pondered. "He also told us growing up that, 'no dream comes true 'til you wake up and go to work.' I think it's a test. Some just join church to conform, to get married, not really putting their whole heart and soul into it. They just sort of hang on like that, doing as little as possible. That's also an empty life. Either way, it's going to take work to live a committed life. And prayer, I think."

The others all nodded their agreement.

Stephen steered the horse along the row of buggies lined up in a field by the barn. Finding a spot, he backed in. No sooner had he stopped than one of the Lapp boys appeared and started unhitching the horse. One of his brothers quickly marked the initials SPT—for Stephen Phoebe Troyer in chalk on the front corner of the buggy in large letters to differentiate it from the others in the field.

"*Denke*, Moses. *Gut* to see you," Stephen said.

"Just leave the horse. I'll get her over by the others. Hope y'all enjoy the evening," he added as he watched curiously as the three decidedly non-Amish girls piled out of the buggy.

Some of Phoebe's close friends came over to greet the girls as they headed toward the barn, Emily among them.

"I'm so glad you came!" she greeted them. "We can sit together and visit, *ya?*"

Phoebe introduced the others to Emily as she shook hands with each one. Together they entered the barn, which appeared packed with every young person from miles around.

"When we get together, it isn't this many," Leah observed.

"Us neither," Susanna commented. Hilde added, "This is such fun. You do this every other week? All year round?"

"Unless the weather is really bad, or we have a funeral and such, *ya*," Phoebe explained.

The others followed Phoebe to a table by the wall and slid into the benches there. The two rows of long tables stretched the length of the barn. Each was set with snacks and drinks down the center of the tables. A stack of *Ausbund* hymn books sat at the ends of each table. All the young people hurried to sit down so they could begin the evening.

Suddenly, five young chaps made a dash for the bench across from Phoebe and the girls, trying to all squeeze into the four places there, crashing into each other in their efforts. Suddenly Phoebe zeroed in on who this bunch were. Phoebe was shocked to see Ben heading the pack of unruly young stallions. Ben, who had been so painfully shy only two years ago, not even that, when Phoebe's parents practically forced her to attend the singing one weekend when she thought she was too busy with school to do anything except study. Ben, who had set his heart on Phoebe—had already fallen hopelessly in love--but had no idea how to express that until it was too late. He'd worried and procrastinated far too long to invite her to ride with him after the singing, missing the opportunity forever. He'd tried to recapture the moment by writing to her, expressing his affection that way, but when there was no response in return, he'd fallen into a hopeless depression. He'd never be able to find the courage to win a girl, any girl.

There was no way to regain his chances with Phoebe now that she was married, but he was still young, he tried to console himself. Only twenty-three now. There were plenty of other fish in the sea, he'd told himself, though there were few others like Phoebe, he fretted. He had finally gone to talk to *Dat*. He was a *gut* help. He'd suggested prayer first. *Gott* already knew who would be the perfect wife for him. *Dat* also reminded him of the old adage, 'the soul could have no rainbows if the eyes had no tears.' *Dat* was sure Ben would find the perfect helpmate, in *Gott's* time, that there was no reason to be morose. That only tempted the bad spirits, not *Gott's Geiste*.

These past two years, Ben diligently worked to overcome his agonizing shyness. He had to tell himself to stand tall, not hunch up his shoulders and duck his head every time he felt challenged. He practiced talking more, looking more confident, at first only in front of his bedroom mirror, and then with others. Little by little, it worked. And he prayed. He prayed in the quiet barn every dawn when he milked the cows. He prayed as he mucked out the stalls, and he prayed most earnestly before he fell asleep every night. Surely *Gott* would hear him. Surely He would help.

Ben managed to get to the bench first, noisily plunking down across from Leah as the other fellows scrambled to find a place on either side of him. He took a deep breath and glanced across the table at Leah. Her eyes were fixed on him. It was obvious. To him, at least. Phoebe noticed it, too. Ben's big brown eyes weren't mooning her way like they had at that singing back two years. He was *staring* at Leah. With his mouth open. And Leah was staring back. *Oh dear,* Phoebe thought to herself. *Not Leah. Oh my. That would be a pickle for sure and for certain. That can't happen. It would break his heart all over again. She's Mennonite, for gosh sakes. He should know she can't date him. What would her family say? What have I started here? Oh Gott, Help!*

One of the older boys stood up when everyone was seated.

"Hi. I'm Eli Lapp. I'll be the song leader tonight. Thanks for all *kumming.* I believe we have some visitors here. Maybe Stephen Troyer can introduce them."

Stephen rose and introduced the girls one by one. Then he added, "They are all students with Phoebe in the nursing program. Thanks for all *kumming,*" he said as he sat down.

Eli called out the page number of the first song, a slow low German hymn traditionally sung at every singing before anyone else could suggest one of the 'fast' songs. Phoebe passed out the glasses and poured soda for those at her table, which they sipped between songs, all the while agonizing over the situation unfolding before her very eyes. Ben barely mouthed the words to the songs, forgetting to turn the pages even. And Leah smiled back at Ben as she continued to look across at him when she wasn't searching for the next hymn that had been announced. She was clearly blushing, though.

Phoebe doubted Leah was worrying about anything else at that moment. The two of them were in their own little world, their own tiny bubble, miles from those right next to them. They had not said a word to each other, yet they were rapidly and deeply falling in love—at first sight. It would be hard to say who was more in love at that moment. He had never felt this kind of love before, but then neither had she. The barn could burn up (or burn down) around them and they wouldn't care. They were absolutely, hopelessly in love. Phoebe was tempted to pinch Leah's thigh under the table and break the spell. Maybe she could frown at her or shake her head and wake her up. She would definitely talk to her if there was a break. Maybe just feign the need to go to the outhouse and beg Leah to go with her. That might work. Then she could talk some sense into her. Before it was too late.

Phoebe caught Susanna's eye just then. She saw the same thoughts in her eyes, that something had to be done. Hilde appeared oblivious to the situation, her gaze roaming across the heads of the young people that filled the barn. Susanna decided to take action. She grabbed Leah's arm and talked into her ear as she bodily lifted her off the bench and left the barn, telling her she needed someone to accompany her to the outhouse. Leah staggered along, still apparently on cloud nine.

"What are you thinking, *dindla?*" Susanna shook her, still holding onto her arm as they headed down the path to the outhouse. "You can't lead that boy on like that. He's Amish. You're Mennonite. Your folks would have a fit! A proper royal purple fit! You haven't even gotten to know him. You can't be thinking that it could work. Please, Leah. You could ruin your family."

Leah didn't respond. She just shook her head, still smiling.

"Wake up, little girl," Susanna begged. "You are encouraging him. It's wrong. It's all wrong."

Leah finally spoke. "Well, we could find a way. Maybe God had this in mind. Maybe we are meant to get to know other Plain people. Maybe we are getting too inbred, you know?"

"No, no. That is not for us to decide. You didn't survive that tornado to break your folks' hearts with this. Think, once. Please," Susanna pleaded. "I need to find the outhouse..." she trailed off, tired of the argument she suspected she wasn't going to win. *Dear*

Lord, how can I make her see? Please give me the right words. How could she fall so hard for this boy? It isn't even love, really. It can't be. Infatuation maybe? It isn't like there aren't boys in her church. Please tell me what to do. Please...

Susanna returned to the barn as the young people finished singing, and were passing around the snacks and visiting. She found Phoebe and Hilde, and their eyes clearly asked her what had happened. She could only shake her head to let them know she couldn't find a way through it, though she'd tried. They went outside together to talk.

"I don't know what's gotten into her. I thought she had her head screwed on right. What could she be thinking?" Susanna asked.

"I know," Phoebe said. "Do you know where she is now?"

Susanna shook her head. "I left her by the barn."

"She didn't come back in," Phoebe said, wringing her hands. "I'll go look in the kitchen."

Susanna and Hilde returned to the barn, sitting down at the table once more, though glancing toward the door periodically to see if they could see her.

"She can't get in too much *mufti* tonight," Hilde reasoned.

"No, I guess not. We'll see her back at Phoebe's anyway," Susanna replied.

Phoebe rejoined them after a while. "I couldn't find her. I expect she'll show up by it's time to leave; we can't babysit. She's grown up."

"You sure of that?" Susanna challenged, her raised eyebrows doubtful.

"I thought I was," Phoebe fretted. *Lord, please keep her safe. Please send your angels to bring her back. Please help her to think straight....*

Chapter Four

After the singing, Phoebe found Stephen who had been sitting with some of his old friends and told him they couldn't find Leah and what had unfolded during the singing.

"Whew. I didn't see that one *kumming* for sure," he said, scratching his newly grown sparse beard.

"Yeah, right?" she replied. "She's clearly playing with fire. What can we do, though?"

"Well, let's just get her home, okay?"

They looked everywhere, collecting Susanna and Hilde along the way. Suddenly, Emily came up to Phoebe.

"Oh, there you are. Leah asked me to tell you that Ben is driving her home. She'll be at your place later."

"Oh, great. You didn't see them, Emily," Phoebe began, "but they're both heading for big trouble."

"Oh, I wouldn't be so worried, Phoebe. They are just friends," Emily stated.

"No, that wasn't a 'just friends' kinda look. They were positively swooning over each other. It's my fault," Phoebe said as she wrung her hands. "It's all my fault."

"*Kumm* on," Stephen finally said, taking her hand. "Let's go home."

They rode home in silence, each shaking their heads in disbelief.

"Oh, I almost forgot. Stephen, we promised we'd go to the Gingerich's tonight just to check in," Phoebe suddenly remembered.

"Okay. Let's go. It's on the way."

Annie met them at the door. "He was able to sip some juice tonight and take his pills. He's quite comfortable and resting now. Our *kinner* are going to stay up with him so I can sleep a bit," she reported.

"Oh, good. Well, I still want you to send Jacob to get me if you need anything tonight, okay? Otherwise, I'll see you tomorrow afternoon if that's alright," Phoebe answered.

"*Ya*, absolutely. Thank you ever so much again," Annie said as she went back into the house.

They arrived home shortly after that.

"I'll wait up for her," Phoebe suggested. "I've got some reading, so I'll do that for a bit. That Coca-Cola has caffeine, doesn't it? That's why I'm still so awake," she said as she grabbed her schoolbag and sat down at the kitchen table. "*Mamm* and *Dat* must have gone to bed. She sure was up early, making that breakfast pizza."

"I still want that recipe," Susanna reminded her. "I'll read for a while too."

Stephen told Phoebe he was going to bed and asked her not to stay up all night. "You don't need to worry, honey. We'll trust *Gott* will show them the right way," he said, patting her arm in lieu of a kiss, which he wouldn't venture in front of the other girls in the kitchen.

Hilde agreed with the others and joined them to study as Phoebe lit another lamp on the end of the kitchen table. "I still can't believe her," Phoebe said, thoroughly disgusted. "I don't know what we can do. Maybe we should just ignore it."

"You think it will just go away then?" Susanna insisted.

"No, but let it die a natural death. They'll just have to see for themselves why it wouldn't work," Phoebe concluded.

The girls read for a while until it was past 1:00 a.m. Finally, Phoebe announced she was going to bed. The others agreed and headed upstairs, Phoebe leading the way with the lamp in her hand. They took turns with the flashlight to visit the outhouse. Finally they were all tucked in bed and dozing off. Phoebe was almost asleep next to Stephen back downstairs when she thought she heard a sound coming from their little *dawdi haus* outer door. There it was again.

She got up and looked out the curtain. Sure enough, there was a buggy at the far end of the drive. *So Leah thought she could sneak in without anyone knowing.*

As Phoebe opened the door, Leah quickly stepped in past her.

"I forgot to bring a flashlight. Can I borrow one? I'm having a rush call to the outhouse," Leah confessed, dancing from one foot to the other. Phoebe found a flashlight and gave it to her, calling in a loud whisper, "I will talk to you in the morning!" as she returned to her bedroom.

Mamm was already busy preparing dinner when Phoebe came down the stairs in the morning.

"Abe and Isaac are *kumming* today, aren't they?" she asked. "I can't wait to see them."

"Me too," *Mamm* said. "I made some oatmeal for breakfast. Can you get out the cream, the granola—I just made a new batch— some canned blueberries and the brown sugar, and maple syrup, oh, and the butter. I'm going to keep going here if you can fix breakfast for the others. *Denke.*"

'The Boys' as *Mamm* and *Dat* still called Abe and Isaac were coming with their families for Sunday dinner. It was a beautiful fall day so the children could play outside. The Four Musketeers would return to college the next morning with Phoebe. They hadn't talked to Leah yet about her lack of judgement the evening before. While Phoebe and *Mamm* were working in the kitchen before the others woke up, she broached the subject, explaining the events at the singing and afterwards.

"And they even rode home together in his buggy, *Mamm*. I just don't know what to do. I feel somewhat responsible—

I mean, I invited her. But in my wildest dreams, I couldn't have planned this. I said something that I thought might be the answer, though. Maybe we should just ignore it and let it die a natural death. I can't imagine it ever working out, anyway. It's not even love, could it really be? More like infatuation. Can that grow into love?"

"It might do," *Mamm* slowly began, pondering this new dilemma. "She'll have enough of her folks going at her, and they'll bring in their minister, and Ben will certainly get an earful from his family, so maybe we don't need to interfere. Maybe it will take care of itself. We must keep them in our prayers, though, that they don't lose their way."

"You're right, of course. *Mamm,* are you okay?" Phoebe asked. "Your face is all red."

"It's just these hot flushes. They aren't as bad as they used to be, but still," she said as she sat down. "I'll just have a drink here and it'll pass."

"I think we should have your blood pressure checked. You haven't had a checkup in quite a while."

"Oh, okay, if you say so," *Mamm* agreed grudgingly.

Phoebe kissed her *mamm*. "I want to keep you around for a *gut* long time. Gotta take care of you. And...well, *Mamm,* it's hot *flashes.* Not flushes."

"You know what I mean!" *Mamm* fussed back at her, disgruntled.

Finally, *Dat* and Stephen came in from their chores just as the girls came down from the upstairs bedroom.

"It's fix-your-own for breakfast," *Mamm* announced. "I'm still working on dinner. Eat first and then I'll let you help me."

"We'll help *Mamm* with dinner right after breakfast," Phoebe announced. "Then we might have an hour or such to study before the boys *kumm. Mamm,* you told them what time?"

"About one o'clock. I got most of the dinner put together yesterday, so it won't take much," she replied. "I made a zucchini pie yesterday with the last zucchini. The *kinner* always gobble that one up, thinking it's apple. And I made more whoopie pies. I was going to make them pumpkin and oats but decided to make chocolate with a raspberry filling. They are *wunderbar-gut*. That 'Cookin' With Maudie' column in *The Budget* for sure has some *gut* ideas."

Catching *Mamm's* eye, Phoebe raised her own eyebrows, questioning if they should address the elephant in the room: Leah's behavior at the singing. *Mamm* immediately knew what Phoebe had in mind but gave a tiny sideways shake of her head that Phoebe recognized in return. *Okay,* she thought to herself. *Maybe it is best to —oh, what is that expression? 'Let sleeping dogs lie.' I just feel so guilty, like I set it up. Dear* Gott, *please tell me if I can fix it, or at least, You fix it somehow. Please, dear Lord....* With that, Phoebe decided not to let it ruin the rest of the girls' visit, and that they should all enjoy their last day.

"What else do you have up your sleeve for today?" *Mamm* asked.

"Nothing much. We'll go to see Annie and Gary before dark, just to pop in. I told her we would," Phoebe explained.

"Did you girls get to work on the quilt at the school yesterday?" *Mamm* asked, attempting to break the silence at the table.

Susanna gulped her coffee and answered first. "It was great. Such a beautiful quilt and I learned how to hand quilt on it. We've always machine quilted ours. It was really fun."

Hilde added, "I liked it so much I'm going to try to hand quilt my next one. I've always admired them that way at the county fair."

"It's takes longer," *Mamm* warned, "but it does look really nice, and I like having friends over to do it all together. That's half the fun."

"That's how I learned," Phoebe said. "Going to quilting bees when I was little. Like we could contribute something, even if our stitches weren't perfect. They were usually too big or horribly uneven, but no one seemed to mind. I bet you unpicked mine later, *Mamm, eh?*"

"We learned to bake that way, too," she continued. "*Mamm* would give us each a little lump of dough when she was baking bread. We'd knead it to death, until it was mushy, and sometimes drop it on the floor and have to dust it off and pick off any cat hairs, and then put it in the oven like that. The boys liked nibbling the raw dough, and *Mamm* would have to give them more dough. But we would think we could really bake and were so excited when we ate those funny misshapen little loaves slathered with jam for lunch afterwards."

"That's how I learned too," Susanna added. "On Friday mornings the bell would ring on the '*hof* and all the mothers and girls would go to the main kitchen to 'hold Friday' with their buckets and cleaning rags and scrub the dining room and kitchen from top to bottom, even emptying out the shelves holding all the dishes and pots and pans and clean it all. I'd bring my little pail and my own rag along and my mom would tie on my little apron and I thought I was just one of them cleaning all morning." Then she asked, laughing, "How many Hutterites does it take to have a work break?" The others all shook their heads, puzzled. "Ten. One to put her feet up and nine to make snack!"

She continued, "Then on Saturday morning, the bell rings and all the mothers and girls go to the kitchen to make Saturday buns—we call them *zwieback*. Every Saturday dinner, we have *clöps und zwieback*—hamburgers and buns. The kitchen sister has all the dough ready and we all roll them and fill up rack after rack of trays and then let them rise again before she bakes them. I got the impression as I got older that Mom would re-roll all my buns, so they looked more like the ones on the trays. When they are done right, each one is supposed to look like a little puckered up kiss underneath."

"You have the same menu all week, week after week?" *Mamm* wondered aloud.

"Yup," Susanna replied. "We've always done it that way from as far back as I can remember. Except one time, the cook forgot to take out the hamburger the night before to thaw it and it had been in the deep freeze, so she made some chicken barbeque we'd canned to eat after butchering with the buns. Boy, you should have seen people's faces when they came into the dining room that day. Especially the *vetter*—the men. One by one they'd walked in, look at the serving dishes on the tables, stop, and then slowly looked at the cook, frowning, before sitting down. It was like she'd committed a mortal sin!"

They all laughed at that. Then Phoebe asked, "So what can we do to help?" She glanced at Leah, who had been especially quiet during breakfast, sitting there grinning like some idiot, still off in her own world. *I'm really worried,* Phoebe thought to herself. *She better snap out of it soon or she's really asking for it. Her family will be at her, for sure.* Gott, *please step in here and help us, please.*

As *Dat* and Stephen set about rearranging the tables and chairs to allow for everyone to be seated together at the table later that day for dinner, the women put the finishing touches on the meal before setting the tables. Stephen came up to Phoebe when they were done and whispered to her,

"*Kumm* with me." She followed him as he led her out of the house and around to their back yard. Sitting there next to the biggest weeping willow in the yard was the sweetest little playhouse she had ever seen, complete with cedar shingles.

"Your *dat* and I have been building it at the furniture barn and brought it over with the horse and the flatbed yesterday."

"It's beautiful! Oh, Stephen. It's for when the *kinner kumm* over here? It's perfect. I love it," she said, hugging him. Looking both ways first, he snuck a kiss before she walked over to the little house and peeked inside. It had windows and a little table and a small bench and a counter with a tiny tea pot and tin cups.

"I can't wait for them to see it," she told him. "Has *Mamm* known?"

"I don't know if he's told her," Stephen answered. They headed back to the kitchen where Phoebe announced, "You've all got to *kumm* and see this." The women wiped their hands on their aprons or a kitchen towel and followed them out to the tiny cottage.

"It's absolutely darling!" Susanna gushed. "I want one!"

"It's so cute," Hilde added. "Our little ones would love something like this. I'll have to tell my dad."

Mamm kept shaking her head, smiling. "Well, if that isn't the cat's mew, I don't know what is."

"Um... *Mamm.* It's 'the cat's me-OW.' Meow, *Mamm,* not mew," Phoebe corrected.

"It's the same exact thing," *Mamm* answered back in her

sternest whisper through gritted teeth and frowned furiously at Phoebe.

"Well, I going to go upstairs to read for a while till they *kumm*," Phoebe announced.

The other girls followed, not wanting to leave their homework till that night. When they got upstairs, Phoebe stood in front of Leah as she flopped onto the cot with her book.

"I don't want to talk about it," Leah said, smiling sweetly. "It's no one else's business, I'll have you know."

"Oh, Leah, please talk some sense. You'd be ruining your lives..." Phoebe began.

"Let's just not talk about it, okay?" Leah demanded and stared down at her book. Phoebe gave up and sat on the big double bed next to Hilde, while Susanna sat in the rocker near the window, opening her textbook, and attempted to read. She had heard what Phoebe said to Leah just then. *I'm too distracted,* she told herself. *Just forget it. You tried. It's in* Gott's *hands now...*

Chapter Five

The girls had fallen asleep over their books, Susanna in the big rocker with her book opened on her lap, the others on the beds. When they heard the buggies approaching, they woke up.

"Hey, get up," Phoebe called. "They're here."

They took turns checking in the mirror on the dresser, licking a finger and swiping it along the edge of their head coverings to tuck in any errant *schtruvvels* (hairs) before heading downstairs.

They met everyone outside as the children kept piling out of the buggies. Susanna tried to count them all and finally gave up as they raced each other to the kitchen to greet their *mammi*.

Phoebe introduced everyone to her brothers and their wives. Some of the children could be heard around the back of the house with Stephen.

"Well, get washed up, you all," *Mamm* said. "I'll call the *kinner*."

When everyone was seated, *Dat,* now *Doddy* (Grandpa) looked at the littlest ones. *"Patties* down?" he asked them. Instantly, all the little hands that had been on the table disappeared onto their laps. So did Susanna's, Hilde's and Leah's. They'd learned the ropes by now after almost three days and obediently followed. *"Gut,* then," he said as he bowed his head for the silent prayer. After a minute or two, he looked up and announced, "Tuck in, then."

The moms had sat down strategically placed to help the littlest ones on either side of themselves. Phoebe introduced the guests to all of the children.

"Why do they look so funny?" four-year-old Gracey asked. Her mother frowned at her.

Susanna answered for the three visitors. "We live in church districts like you do, but we have different *tract*," she explained. "Not so very different, really."

"Why does your scarf have all those dots?" Eliza asked.

"Let our guests eat their dinner," their *mamm* replied.

"I don't mind," Susanna said. "It's just a very old tradition from Moravia. My great-great-great-great grandmothers all wore them this way." Turning to Phoebe and chuckling, she added, "Once we had a visitor, a professor who was writing about our colony, who actually asked what the dots all meant. I was a teenager then, and I told him that each one represents a struggle I'd been through. He believed me, too!" That brought laughs all around. "My mom said I should have told him that 'the more dots you have, or the bigger the dots, the more up in seniority you are in the community,' and just let him think about that for a while."

Hilde spoke up next. "I once told my cousin Sam that they'd taken the word 'gullible' out of the dictionary; that it was old-fashioned and wasn't used anymore. He said, 'really?' and I told him yes. He said, 'wow, I'll have to tell my *dat* about this.'"

The younger children hadn't understood the joke, but the older ones did and laughed, shaking their heads.

"That's a *gut* one," *Dat* said, laughing harder than anyone else.

"Another time," Susanna added, "a visitor, a sociology student, who was also studying us or whatever, doing research, asked very diplomatically at dinner why there wasn't a mirror in the bathroom, thinking it was part of the *Ordnung* or some theological point. My *mudder* tried not to laugh when she told him, 'well that's because the boys had a fight in there the other day and broke it and father hasn't replaced it yet.'"

"How many *kinner* in your families?" Avram asked the guests.

"Eleven in mine," Susanna answered, which elicited a whistle from Viktor. His dad frowned at him then for the blatant indiscretion.

"Not at the table, Viktor," he corrected.

"Three in mine," Hilde continued.

Leah was still spacing out where she sat, pushing her sweet potatoes around her plate in a circle for the second time, sitting by Phoebe, who nudged her with her elbow. "How many kids in your family?" Phoebe posed the question to her again.

"Oh, four brothers and me," she answered, looking up momentarily, that other-worldly expression still plastered on her face.

"I should introduce ours, shouldn't I?" Abe asked and then began.

"This is Avram, and next to him is Gracey. Then Viktor, next is Verity, Willa, and Fiona is holding Harley. Your turn, Ike," Abe said to his brother.

"Oh, okay," he began. "My wife is Hannah Mary and next to her is Rhoda, who is holding Amos, then there's Ivy and Sol."

During a lull in the conversation Willa addressed Susanna who was sitting next to her. Willa had been studying her for the past few minutes. Willa was almost five.

"You're fat," Willa pronounced.

"Willa!" her mother scolded, turning beet red.

"It's okay," Susanna answered, then looking down at Willa, she said, "I know. I must like to eat lots of cakes, eh?"

Willa nodded.

"I love to bake cookies and Danish, too. Maybe I should walk more, huh?" Susanna suggested.

Willa nodded again. The other children were laughing, so Willa took their cue and smiled before going back to her dinner, while her parents were still shaking their heads, totally mortified, not laughing or even smiling.

"How many horses does your *dat* have?" Luke asked Susanna.

"We don't have any," she answered.

"Huh? How's that? Don't you go to church or anywhere?" Sol asked.

Susanna explained: "We live in a community like yours, but we use cars, like some of the more progressive churches. We don't each own one. They belong to the community, they are all shared. We don't have TVs or radios, but some things are different. Like my dad has two hundred hogs. It's actually a huge farm with all the dads in our colony working there together."

"Wow! I'd like to see that," one of the children commented. "Can we visit sometime? Please?"

Abe answered for their guests, "that would be fun, eh? Maybe we can sometime."

Then Ike spoke up. "I've been thinking. Our school has a spelling bee at the end of every year. Wouldn't it be fun to invite their school to compete? We could look into that, huh?"

Susanna jumped at the idea. "That would be such fun. I will ask when we get home. Oooh. I like that idea! And maybe you could come to our open house at Christmas when we invite all the neighbors to sing the Messiah together. You might really enjoy that." Then, taking Willa into her confidence again, she whispered to her, "I get to make *tons* of Christmas cookies for the refreshments at the open house. We start Christmas baking in September. You'd like that, huh?"

Again, Willa nodded vigorously.

"What kinds?" Ivy wanted to know.

"Lots. You want me to name them all?" Susanna asked. Ivy and Willa both nodded.

"Oh, Ivy, let her eat!" Isaac scolded.

"It's okay," she replied. "I'll make fruit cake first because we like it to age a bit in the cooler. Then there's mincemeat—it's inside a sugar cookie, and molasses shortbreads," she said counting off on her fingers. "Let's see, then there's turtle cookies, Russian wedding cakes, *pfeffernusse* and *lebkuchen, butterkekse, spekulatius*—which is an anise cookie you dip in your coffee or cocoa—*lebkuchen* that we ice with almond glace, *acahner printen, weckmännchen, zimtsterne* and *aakronen* with marzipan. I don't know the names in English. You'll just have to come and try them, huh?"

The children all nodded at that and Phoebe noticed Abe and Isaac nodding slightly too, probably quite unconsciously.

After dinner, the children raced back outside again while the others cleaned up the kitchen. The boys replaced the tables before going outside, too.

Fiona came up to Susanna and apologized profusely for Willa's indiscretion.

"Oh, don't worry. She's a dear. I love how honest the little ones are," Susanna said.

"I know," Fiona added, laughing too as she dried the dishes with Susanna.

Close to four o'clock, Stephen reminded Phoebe they still had to visit the Gingerichs. They found Hilde inside the new playhouse, surrounded by little girls serving tea. They found Leah after searching everywhere, in a corner of the living room, dozing in a large rocking chair.

"She got in pretty late," Phoebe commented to Stephen as she gently rocked the chair.

"Time to get up, sleepy head," Phoebe cooed.

"Oh. What are we doing now?" Leah asked, stretching her arms and legs out.

"We told the Gingerichs we'd be by. Then home. School tomorrow," Phoebe reminded her.

"Oh, sorry," Leah began. "I forgot to tell you. Ben is picking me up at five. We won't see each other all week till next weekend otherwise," she explained while looking at the floor and bracing for the retort she was sure would come, trying to foil their plans.

"You have got to be kidding me! Really?" Phoebe fumed. "*REALLY?* This won't work. It just won't."

Stephen stepped in at this point, placing his hand on his wife's shoulder. "They'll figure that out, hon. Let them find out on their own."

"But you have a *date* with him?" Phoebe asked incredulously.

Leah rose from the chair and headed out to the outhouse.

"Yeah, we'll figure it out, trust me," she called back over her shoulder as she left, avoiding eye contact at all cost.

"Okay," Stephen said to Phoebe as they watched her leave. "Drop it. You'll never win. They will have a rude awakening one of these days. You can't fix it, Pheebs."

"You're right," she conceded. "You're always right," she said as she kissed him, wrapping her arms around his waist. She rested her head against his chest. He had to bend down but managed to hug her firmly in return. "Mmmmm," she hummed, relaxing into her wise old man. Dat *is always right,* was her *mamm's* old adage. *Except when he's not,* she thought to herself, slightly amused.

Chapter Six

The rest visited Annie and Gary for a while. He was about the same, sleeping a bit more, and his breathing had become shallower. Jacob and Stephen visited outside while the girls were inside. Finally, Phoebe, Hilde and Susanna came out to join them.

"He's about the same," Phoebe reported. "I'll stop by after school tomorrow but do get me if there's anything you need tonight, please," she said, addressing Jacob.

"I will," he agreed.

They drove home in silence until Phoebe again started fretting about Leah once more. "How can she?" she asked again.

"Leave it," Stephen gently counselled, taking her hand in his after shifting the reins to his left hand. "I bet it will die a quiet death in a matter of weeks. Just wait. Maybe it will make them a little wiser when it's all said and done. I don't know."

"Well, they've both got their heads in the sand. They better get ready for a rude awakening. They were made for each other for certain, dumb ostriches," she fumed.

"Maybe, just maybe, it was meant to be," Susanna offered. "He could become Mennonite, couldn't he? Or she could become Amish? Is it allowed? Has it ever happened that you know of?"

"It could be mighty tough going. Just getting past the families would test them to the limit," Hilde added.

"Leave her be. You girls have enough to worry about. School tomorrow, finals in May, then your boards, and graduation in June. You have plenty on your plates. Don't let her ruin it for you, huh?" Stephen sagely advised.

"Okay," Phoebe agreed.

"Yeah," Hilde and Susanne conceded.

"You could even be kind," Stephen mused. "She was a *gut* friend. There's a saying, 'kill them with kindness.' Maybe don't just cut her off. She'll need friends. *Gut* friends if they're going to be tackling this one. Let her know you'll support her whatever. It's really in *Gott's* hands now."

"Well," Susanna began. "That is one way of looking at it. What do you think?" she asked, looking at the others.

"I guess," Phoebe ventured grudgingly.

"I agree," Hilde said. "I wouldn't want it for all the world, but then I'm not her."

They came into the kitchen just as *Mamm* was lighting the lamps. The soft glow that slowly spread throughout the house never ceased to bring with it a kind of familiar peace—holy even— if one took the time to acknowledge it. This glow brought the evening when perhaps nature meant us to relax, gather, and end the work of the day. It signaled bedtime and stories for the children and warm cocoa or hot milk with honey. It brought with it a time to breathe in, to let go of all the strain and stresses that the day had demanded, replacing it with a blanket of harmony, calm and tranquility, if you let it.

It wasn't bright enough to quilt or embroider by, though some could still knit, but mending black pants was practically impossible at night. More frugal Amish homes would only light the lamps in one room until bedtime, forcing everyone in that house to gather there, which was the case tonight.

"Anyone for Rummykub?" *Mamm* asked enthusiastically.

Phoebe groaned. "*Mamm*, we have to study, just for a bit. Sorry."

Dat was reading *The Budget* in his chair under the mantle lamp hanging close by.

"Listen to this one," he read as the girls opened their books at the table. ""Cookin' With Maudie' has a recipe for Dandelion

49

Omelet, sent in by someone named something...uh...Schwartz in Indiana. I don't know 'em. Yuck. Don't you dare try that, *Mamm*," he ordered.

"And here's one for something called 'Frito Pies' from someone in Ohio." He continued to read out loud, "'Heat up the chili, cut off the tops of the Frito snack packs, spoon in the chili, add a spoon and eat. Very good and hardly any dishes to wash.' What is this world *kumming* to?" he asked out loud to no one in particular. "Can you believe it? Now, can you?"

A few minutes later, he called out. "This is from Pennsylvania. It says, 'Birthdays are nice, especially for four-year-olds. 'It's fit to be four, a lot more fun than being three!' little Mervin told his dad. When he was asked what he wanted for his birthday supper, he answered without hesitation, 'A cake!' 'What else do you want?' they asked him. 'Well, frosting,' he said. 'No, what do you want for something *hot*?' his dad asked him again. 'Candles,' he answered. Cake was it for him, I guess.'"

"Aw. That's precious," Susanna answered.

Mamm was busy puttering at the kitchen counter. "Well, I'm ready to go to bed. See you all in the morning," she said as she headed toward their room, the Rummykub box safely tucked back in the games cupboard.

"Don't stay up too late," she added.

The girls studied for another two hours and finally agreed they'd quit there. Leah wasn't home yet.

As Phoebe was just dozing off, she heard the door rattling again like the night before. She'd left it unlocked and hung a flashlight on the handle where Leah couldn't miss it. Sure enough, she heard her come in and fumbling found her way up the stairs.

In the morning, *Mamm* had breakfast ready early. The girls were enjoying their breakfast tortillas, compliments of Maudie's column in *The Budget* once again. *Mamm* came to the table as *Dat* and Stephen arrived from the barn. She set down four brown paper lunch bags. "I made you some lunch," she told the girls.

"Oh, thank you so much," Susanna said. "You didn't have to do that. That's so sweet. Thanks."

"Thanks a lot," Hilde added.

"Well, that school cafeteria must charge a fortune for a *gut* lunch, and I had plenty left over from dinner yesterday," *Mamm* explained. "Enjoy it," she added.

"Thank you so much," Leah said. "It's been a really good weekend. You can have a rest from all of us now."

"It was a pleasure," *Mamm* replied, studying Leah a moment longer, wondering at what the dear girl thought she was embarking on. *It sure won't be easy, Mamm* thought to herself. *She's going to hurt a few people, maybe get herself or get that boy excommunicated, shunned. Their poor* mamms. *I for certain wouldn't know what to do if I were her* mamm. *Poor thing. Why do some make their lives so very complicated? Dear* Gott, *please go with them. Dear Lord....*

The others were tempted to say something to Leah but decided against it, hoping Stephen's wisdom from the previous night would suffice.

"What are we studying today, I wonder?" Phoebe said, changing the subject.

"It's a full moon tonight," Hilde added. Then, addressing *Mamm,* she asked, "Some say more babies are born on the full moon. Do you think that's so?"

Mamm answered, "Well, might be. Babies know when to get born without us having much to do with it, though."

"Mamm," Phoebe began, "I will be stopping by the Gingerich's after school today. Some *mamms* want me to help them with their medical questions. Lord knows I can't really do anything for them, but I'll listen. I am thinking that I should maybe stay the night and support Annie. Gary won't be with us much longer." She turned to Stephen then.

"Stephen, maybe don't expect me tonight. I will get Mr. Schrock to bring me home or take me to school in the morning from there, depending on how it goes." Stephen nodded back to her while finishing his coffee.

"That's fine. I'll be keeping him in prayer, you can tell Annie," *Mamm* said.

"I will, for sure," Phoebe promised. Then she took a closer look at her tortilla, slowly turning it so she could see into each end. She laid it back down on her plate and carefully unrolled it.

"Mamm," she began tentatively. "Why are the scrambled eggs red? And are the hash-browns...green?"

"Ummm..." *Mamm* hesitated. "Well, ah, see, yesterday, I decided to color all of my wooden spoons. I've looked at drab wooden spoons for over forty years. I got out the food coloring and did all of them. It seems to come off on the food just a little bit when I'm cooking, I guess," *Mamm* admitted sheepishly.

"But *Mamm,* that is permanent. It's food coloring. We'll have red eggs forever!" Phoebe exclaimed, and at the same time saw *Dat* and Stephen silently chuckling behind their hands. Susanna and Hilde were looking into their tortillas, obviously horrified, their furrowed eyebrows saying everything. Leah continued chewing, oblivious to their banter.

Dat couldn't hide it another moment and laughed out loud, slapping the table. "I suppose the mashed potatoes will be blue next," he chuckled, shaking his head and tilting his chair backwards. "You could always write and tell Maudie about your red eggs and blue mashed potatoes. I bet they'd print that."

Stephen tried to be a bit more respectful of his mother-in-law. "Well, it's a change, for sure," he ventured optimistically.

Chapter Seven

Mr. Schrock arrived right on time early Monday morning to drive the girls to school. They loaded their bags into the trunk and were off.

"Thanks so much, Phoebe," Susanna began. "That was quite the weekend."

"It was lovely," Hilde added. "I can't wait to tell my family all about it."

"Hmmm," Leah offered by way of an agreement with their thanks.

The car was soon at the college and they all piled out, ready for another week closer to graduation. The class, which had begun more than a year ago with over thirty students was now down to almost half, just fourteen. One by one, girls dropped out for as many reasons. Those left behind felt especially challenged to work harder and not cause reason for even a point to be deducted from their grades for any infraction, no matter how minor.

Entering the classroom, Phoebe noticed two girls standing by their desks, apparently waiting for the Plain contingent to arrive. Norma and Steff were wearing long white skirts, much like the ones The Four Musketeers had created for themselves when the class began going into the hospital for the clinical phase of their training. The Plain girls were dumbstruck, stopped dead in their tracks, gawping with their mouths open as the two students giggled.

Norma explained, "We liked your dresses so much, we made ones for ourselves this weekend. I think they turned out quite nice, don't you?"

Steff added, "Don't look so shocked, ladies. We need a bit of fun around here, don't you think?"

"We made the tops from a scrub top pattern to match. Pretty cool, huh?" Norma added.

"They're beautiful," Phoebe exclaimed, still amazed at their initiative, neither of them being any part of a Plain church to her knowledge. "Now you just need a white *kapp,*" she teased, smiling.

"Uh, no, this is as far as I go," Steff replied, laughing.

"I would wear one," Norma said, apparently serious, testing the others.

"Really?" Susanna asked, incredulously.

"Yeah. I'd like that," Norma said. To Phoebe, she actually sounded sincere.

"I could bring you one..." Phoebe slowly offered, though tentatively.

"I would wear it," Norma insisted, as the teacher came into the classroom. Phoebe nodded slightly at Norma as she took her seat.

Phoebe stayed after class, hoping to speak to the teacher.

"I have been helping an older couple in my community," she began. "He's dying and wanted to be at home at the end, so we brought him home. It's been close to three weeks, but I don't think he'll last more than a couple of more days. I'm just wondering if there is anything else I can do. I feel so unprepared, though Annie, his wife, seems better at these kinds of things than I am. She cared for her mom at home when she passed away. Do you have any suggestions?" Phoebe pleaded.

The teacher smiled and nodded on her way to the tall cupboard by her desk, chose a small book, and handed it to Phoebe. "I think you should read this. It's a good one. Your grades are great, so I'm assigning you the book to read tonight, instead of that essay I wrote on the board today for homework. Okay? It's one of Elisabeth Kübler-Ross' earlier ones, and one of my own favorites."

"Oh, thanks so much. You're the best. Thank you!" Phoebe replied, taking the book.

That evening Mr. Schrock drove Phoebe to the Gingerich's. On the way, Phoebe read as much of the book as she could manage, skimming as fast as she could.

"Homework?" Mr. Schrock asked, which was rare for him. He often didn't say much of anything while he drove.

"Yes. I'm trying to finish this one tonight," she replied without looking up.

They arrived soon after, and Phoebe explained to him that if he could wait, she'd check with Annie and see if she should stay the night or not. Going into the kitchen, Annie met her, smiling as usual, in spite of the somber atmosphere.

"No, you don't need to stay tonight. His sister is here from Ohio. Plenty visiting and helping me, *denke,*" Annie said, patting Phoebe's hand. "It's hard, watching him like this, it never gets easy, but he is so peaceful. We could never thank you enough for helping us bring him home. We will always be grateful." Annie hugged her before Phoebe went back out to the car.

The next morning, Phoebe picked out one of her starched organdy *kapps* and carefully folded it into a clean *ditchly* and tucked it into her book bag. She grabbed some white bobby pins and a couple of ponytail elastic bands and stuck those into her purse as well. Once she arrived at the classroom, she signaled Norma to follow her to the ladies' room.

"I'm so excited!" Norma exclaimed.

"Hold still," Phoebe insisted as she twisted Norma's shoulder-length hair into a bun, securing it with the elastic bands. Then shaking out the *kapp,* she set it over the back of Norma's head, announcing, "there, that's just right," she said, pinning it into place. The two giggled as they looked into the large mirror, dressed so similarly, Norma smiling from ear to ear.

"Gosh. Do I look like the real thing?" Norma asked.

"Well, *eh*...you would if you took off the lipstick and green eye shadow," Phoebe commented wryly.

"Oh, okay," Norma agreed, quickly wetting a paper towel and removing the makeup. "Let's go."

As they took their seats, the teacher stopped what she was doing and looked back and forth between the two of them. Finally she asked, "Norma, have you converted or... uh... something?"

Both girls broke into giggles, along with half the class. All Norma could do at that point was nod her head.

"Well, then, um, let's go to the next chapter, page three-hundred-forty," the teacher said, still quite baffled.

Later, The Four Musketeers met at their usual table for lunch.

"That was a hoot," Susanna said once they were all assembled. "I love it!"

Phoebe took a sip of her coffee and then said, "Look, she's coming in for lunch. It would look okay if she didn't have those LED flashing lights sneakers. What would the bishop ever say?" she laughed, attempting to take another sip of coffee, and then snorted, coughing coffee all over her sandwich.

"*Ya*, that doesn't quite work, does it?" Hilde commented. "Those things even come with a remote so you can change the colors, did *ya* know?"

"She's brave. You think she's interested in being Plain?" Susanna asked.

"I doubt it," Phoebe said, wiping her place off with a paper napkin. "But she's just genuine. I like her. You see what you get."

"Yeah, she'll make a good nurse, too. She's smart. I'm surprised she's not going for her RN," Hilde continued. "Do you think she still might?"

"I bet," Phoebe replied. "She could be a doctor if she tried. She could do anything she put her mind to."

Phoebe had been watching Leah all morning, too. She was still as aloof as she'd been over the weekend. Phoebe wondered what was going on with her. How could she ask without further alienating her former friend? *I wonder if she told her parents yet. I bet the sparks will fly then. I'm guessing they're still determined to make this work somehow, though I can't imagine how. Maybe Emily can clue me in. Surely Ben's said something at home. I can go by her place after school, even stay overnight. We used to have sleepovers all the time when we were teenagers. I'll let* Mamm *know...* she planned in her thoughts. *I'll go tomorrow night.* She made a mental note to arrange it with Mr. Schrock today when he picked her up.

Part Two

Chapter Eight

Ben and Leah had been furiously writing back and forth since they'd met at the singing only a week ago. Every day, in fact. The ride home in the buggy was far too short to say everything they wanted to say. Even the date the next evening wasn't long enough to tell each other everything they wanted to share, even though he dropped her off at Phoebe's, where she was staying, close to two a.m.

The conversation on that last night had become complicated. They tried to imagine all sorts of scenarios, whittling down their options. The facts were daunting: Ben was Amish. Leah was Mennonite. They were both of age in their communities to join church, but had not made that life commitment yet, leaving them free to date, but not for long. A commitment to their respective ways of life was expected soon after their *rumschpringe* 'running around' or teen years, and definitely required before marriage in either Plain group.

Their date that night had quickly gone from holding hands to *schmunzling*, which the majority of Plain churches reserved exclusively for marriage. Some more conservative groups even forbade hand holding until the couple were properly engaged, and then quickly married off before the spirit became even weaker than the flesh. The fact that their love was this intense and passionate, and that they felt they were inseparable, eternally destined to be together, had excluded any possibility that this could be wrong. But it was. It was wrong in the eyes of their elders, their churches, their families, their entire lives thus far as ordained by God. They had blatantly rejected their churches' norms for dating, that they should rather get to know one another 'from afar' before things became emotional, even physical, clouding their better judgement, sure to tempt one to sin, never mind they weren't even from the same denomination.

But the young don't always see things that way. They see what's basically forbidden as a challenge, not an obstacle. An exciting, once-in-a-lifetime invitation to gamble, to challenge the status quo and the powers that be, to taunt fate. It was often the subject of sermons: warnings to instill fear in any who would dare to dabble in concert with Satan. Such sermons might even name those who had left the fold, who married whom against everyone's better judge- ment, how their lives were now a disaster or ended in divorce, sullying any future opportunities for chaste happiness, that God would not bless such a union and that there would be dire divine consequences. They had both heard it all and chose to reject such wisdom, beliefs they thought had been borne of an antiquated faith attempting to govern through fear.

Their options were tempting and there appeared to be plenty. The two had spent sleepless nights mulling over each possibility and its alternative scenario. To begin with, Leah offered to become Amish and join Ben's church. Or Ben could conceivably become Mennonite and join Leah's church. Or they could both leave and join a more progressive group, many of which were springing up all over the country, though they could both be shunned by their fami- lies and home communities for doing so, according to the *Ordnung* currently being adhered to by each church.

Joining either church might require months or even years of testing before becoming eligible for church membership, the deci- sion resting both with the entire congregation and the hierarchy, including members who might feel such conversions unacceptable. On top of that, when members voted, it had to be unanimous to result in a positive outcome. We are not talking about democracies here. Some believed that one should not veer from where God had placed them at birth, evidently proclaiming His Will for them to remain there for life.

The more far-fetched alternatives were also to be considered. They could leave Plain life altogether and marry in the *Englische* world, though that was not a first choice for either of them but could be considered should all else fail. That could conceivably leave them, however, with the consequence of both being automatically cut off forever from their families and friends. Neither felt equipped to enter into the outside world, lacking the skills and education they knew were needed for such a transition. The magnitude of that option was beyond anything they could fathom. They could not imagine life without any support of any kind.

Ben only had an eighth-grade education, which had not prepared him for much else beyond what he already knew. The fact that the communities educated their children only so far had obviously been adopted prior in an effort for young people to refrain from leaving. Other edicts had been similarly calculated to foil any attempts at desertion of The True Way by those who genuinely believed God had indeed called each individual to remain faithful. But this option was not yet rejected entirely.

On the other hand, Leah would have her LPN license in a matter of months. That could count for something. Ben could hire himself out to any of the large farms or factories that were always advertising for positions. They could also appropriate the skills they have already that other renegades had found successful out in the world. There are bustling restaurants in Pennsylvania, Minnesota, Wisconsin, Ohio and other places promising authentic Amish cuisine.

There was the entire tourist industry, including B&Bs, bakeries, furniture stores and gift shops touting Amish wares that are not necessarily run by Amish folks. Some were even known to stoop so low as to dress up their *Englische* waitresses in Amish *tract* to look authentic and draw tourists.

Their letters to each other continued to explore whatever their young minds could imagine life might offer for them as a couple. They were excited, scared, exhilarated and wildly, youthfully optimistic, not to mention naive. It seemed to each that the sky was the limit. Their futures didn't have to mirror the daily, monotonous grind of their parents.

Monday, October 1ˢᵗ

Dear Leah,

Greetings of love in our Dear Lord's Name!

I sure enjoyed our date last night. Hope you did too. I can't believe how we met, can you? It was like it was always meant to be. I haven't told my family anything yet, though my sister Emily suspects something, I think. She knew I had asked to drive you home after the singing last Saturday. She hasn't mentioned it, though. I wonder if she told Mamm or Dat about that. Nobody has said anything. I probably have to say something soon. I think I will wait till later in the week. I figured out that I could get a bus to Rice Lake next Saturday and we could spend the day together if you want. I could just tell them I have a date. They won't have to ask lots of questions. They would wonder with who, but that's okay for now. Or you could get a ride here, though I am afraid too many people would notice. Maybe somewhere halfway between for both of us? Your college is too far to drive the buggy, so we'll have to think of something for the weekend. I can't imagine not seeing you every weekend. Maybe you have some gut *ideas? Let me know. All I know is that I have never been happier in my whole life. Don't lose courage.*

P.S. I could give my letters for you to Phoebe to deliver at your school, but I don't want her spoiling it for us. Not yet.

With all my love and prayers,
   Ben

Leah's letter crossed Ben's in the mail. He received it Tuesday morning. His *mamm* had laid it at his place at the table before dinner that day. Of course, she was curious. He had rarely received mail at all, usually only on his birthday and then only from cousins and aunts and uncles who took pity on him and tried to surround him with their love and care.

As he sat down, he noticed the letter. He immediately looked at the return address label. It was from her. Yes! It had to be her. He lifted his plate slightly and shoved it underneath, though he knew he couldn't make the incriminating evidence completely disappear. *Mamm* was too clever for that. Sure enough, after the silent grace, she broached the subject.

"Who wrote?" she asked outright.

"Oh, just a friend I met at the singing," he answered honestly.

"Anyone I know?" she persisted.

"Maybe," was all he could think to say.

"Try me," was the immediate retort.

"I am just getting to know her. I promise if things get serious I'll tell *ya,* okay? Please don't start bugging me."

"Fair enough," his *mamm* replied. Good. He had put that hurdle to rest. For now, at least. She was taken aback that he had even defended himself as much as he had and warded her off at all.

The second the meal was over, he jumped up, grabbed the letter while taking his plate and glass to the sink and made a beeline for his bedroom. Ripping open the envelope, he read,

October 1

Dear Ben,

I hope this letter finds you well. I have been on cloud nine ever since we met. I could not have imagined this in my wildest dreams. I think God has arranged this, don't you? I keep thinking what we should do. I hope you have some ideas. I have a few, but there's so much to consider and I don't know which one is right.

I have school all week. I could send my letters home to you with Phoebe who lives in your settlement, but I know she won't give them to you. She's still not very happy with me. I think she blames herself for us meeting. She shouldn't, you know. Not if God planned it all. Nothing can stop us if He ordained it, right? She could bring your letters to me at school, too. No, she wouldn't. She doesn't approve. Miss Prissy.

I don't know how we can meet on the weekends. Maybe you could get a driver and meet me near here and tell your folks you're dating someone from another district from yours and they wouldn't automatically think I wasn't Amish. I wonder if I could do that—join your church. It would sure be different, but I could. It would have to be for the rest of my life. That's a big one. It would be just as hard for you to become Mennonite, but maybe easier than for me. I just don't know. How long would it take for me to convert? Would they even accept that, knowing I was doing it just to get married? I think it might be easier for you coming here. I haven't told anyone, though Hilde goes to my church. I asked her not to say anything, but you know how girls gossip. I don't want my parents hearing it through the grapevine. I wish I could give my letters for you to Phoebe at school, but I know she's not in agreement yet. Oh, I wish everyone would just mind their own business. Everyone here thinks they have to know what everyone else is doing. It drives me crazy. Can't they just be happy for us? Why can't they?

I send this with all my love,
  Leah

Ben still had chores to finish but told himself he would write back to her later that evening, putting it in the mailbox with the flag up first thing in the morning. *Mamm* wouldn't think to snoop in the mailbox. It was a long driveway, and she didn't relish long walks, anyway. She hardly made it upstairs every day to clean. With the extra weight she'd put on with each *kinner,* she wasn't going to be training for a marathon anytime soon.

She'd tried diets. All the latest health fads made it into her sisters' circular letters. She'd tried them all, they all had: Atkins, Keto, Paleo, South Beach, Weight Watchers, Zone, even a raw diet. Raisin cookies made with monk fruit in a dehydrator and tasted like cardboard. And then she thought to herself that if *Gott* made all these yummy foods, why couldn't she eat them, even enjoy them? Maybe it was just her fate to be pleasantly plump. No one wants a skinny wife now, do they? She thought back then to the funny plaque she had seen in her friend Penelope's kitchen. It read:

"A plump wife and a big barn never did any man harm." So then and there she decided it wasn't too bad staying plump.

He carried his milking pail and stool up to the first cow, pushing the hay away beneath her back legs with his boot, sat down and then wiped her udders with the disinfectant-soaked sponge from his other bucket. Positioning the sterile pail, he began milking.

"Well, Muffin," he said to the cow, who was placidly chewing hay in her stanchion. "What should I write?" He began, gathering his thoughts as the steady *p'chew-ping, p'chew-ping* sounds of the milk squirting hit against the sides of the metal pail and tattooed in his ears. "Isn't she the most beautiful thing on earth? I can't imagine my life without her. I think I said that enough the other night that she believes me. I don't know what we're gonna do, though. I know *Dat* might have some ideas, he's smart like that, but I don't know where this'll stand with him. He might be against it, or *Mamm* might make him against it. She'd want me to stay on the farm, marry here, and give her lots of grandchildren. That's what she'd want. Cut and dried. Just like hay."

Ben picked up his stool and the two buckets and moved to the next cow, setting up to milk her.

"Chocolate, do you have any *gut* ideas?" he asked, addressing the black Angus cow looming above him. He had named her when he was eleven, thinking the little black calf he loved so much would produce chocolate milk when she grew up, but of course, she gave only white milk, much to his disappointment. He patted her sleek side, signaling he was ready. "I should write a letter when I'm done here in the barn. I could tell her about my idea of breaking Amish, going Mennonite. Maybe since I didn't join church here before I leave I wouldn't be put in the *Bann* and we could *kumm* back and visit all the time with our *kinner*, too. I dunno. I'll ask *Dat*. I think she's *wunderbar*, though. She's so smart, too. Not like me. But she says she don't care about that. And maybe her *dat* would find me work over there, enough to take care of a family. I'd do just about anything to make this work. I bet they have cows, too. Probably the latest milking machines, besides."

By the time Ben had milked Cupcake, their brown Guernsey, the last of the cows in the barn, and hauled the milk to the dairy room, he'd thought up the perfect letter. He kicked off his barn boots in the mud room outside the kitchen and proceeded to wash up. The sun was at the horizon, the evening growing dim. His *mamm* was lighting the lamps. Before she could accost him with any more questions, he ran up the stairs two at a time to his room, lit the lamp on the small table there and began his letter.

Tuesday, Oct. 2

My dear Leah,

Greeting of love in our Dear Lord's Name!

I hope you are well and not studying too hard, though I know you are so you can graduate in June. I sure wouldn't want to go back to school. I barely made it through eighth grade. But I will do anything to take care of our family. I am thinking maybe your father can find me a job there. There's lots I can do, and I'd work real hard, just not something that has to do with books.

They're talking about butchering the hogs soon. Right after we cut the last hay. Before we know it, it'll snow. I hope you like to skate 'cause I do. We can hitch up the sleigh and go for sleigh rides, too. I am wondering if you know how someone converts to be Mennonite? I guess I might have to read a bunch of books about it, but I'd do anything for you. Even that. You know that. I think. I hope.

I've been thinking, how would your folks take it if you became Amish? Just wondering. I still don't know what to do. Maybe after my dat knows about us a while I could ask him. I don't think he's ready yet. Not sure. I might kind of feel out what he thinks first.

Please don't worry about my bad spelling. Hopefully, we won't have to write to each other for the rest of our lives. That would be awful. I'm sure Gott will help us. I am sure prayin' and askin' for help. Keep your courage up. I love you. I always will.

Ben

Leah had already been mulling over their predicament when Ben's letter arrived. She excused herself early that evening and went to her room to write down some of her thoughts. Sharing everything with Ben had brought them even closer. They were both grateful how easily it had become to talk and write what was on their hearts.

Dearest Ben, October 3

Thank you for your lovely letter which arrived just today. I think about you all the time, but your letters are so extra special. I am so grateful for how we can trust each other. If we can do that for the rest of our lives, we'll have a pretty strong marriage, I hope.

This whole converting thing has me puzzled. Why would everyone be so upset by it? I once heard a sermon where the visiting minister started out by stating the following: 'There are many Christians throughout the world, but very few followers of Christ.' I've never forgotten that. So if we are choosing a committed life for Jesus, does it matter so much where or how we do that? We have a free will and a conscience, so if we pray about things, we should be given a direction from Him, right? I will have to ask our minister that one. He is pretty open. I don't know what he will say, though.

Have you told your family yet? I haven't. Maybe if I see you on the weekend we can discuss how to do that. It scares me a bit. I just don't want a fight, ya know? I know we must honor our father and mother, but are there any times we can't or shouldn't? When we are adults? How does that work?

Well, I have to study and then to bed. I've started a quilt for us. I only work on it when we are visiting downstairs in the family, so it's slow going. I can't get behind in my schoolwork. See you soon. I love you more each day.

Yours forever,
   Leah

Chapter Nine

Phoebe had arranged to visit Emily after school the next day. Mr. Schrock had another trip in the area that evening, so he offered to pick her up and bring her home later. When Phoebe arrived, Ben was in the barn with his *dat*. Emily was in the kitchen fixing a simple supper with her *mamm* and three younger siblings were at the kitchen table coloring pictures that they would send to their *grossmammi* who was in the hospital with a broken hip, to cheer her up.

"*Mamm,* if you are okay here, I'll visit with Phoebe a bit before supper," Emily suggested.

"*Ya,* go. Don't go too far. It will be ready by six," *Mamm* said.

The girls went out to the porch and sat together on the swinging bench.

"Has he said anything?" Phoebe asked Emily.

"Well, he knows that I know because I was there at the singing. And *Mamm* knows something's up cause he gets mail almost every day but won't tell her who's writing. And he got picked up by a driver last Saturday and went somewhere and won't tell us, but I know they are getting together. He tells *Mamm* and *Dat* that he'll clue them in if it gets serious, but that can only put them off for so long. I cornered him the other day and told him that he has got to talk to them, that he can't just run away or do something stupid. He agreed to that and said he'd talk to *Dat* soon."

Phoebe filled Emily in. "Leah won't talk about it at school, so we really don't know much. I've talked to my *mamm* but made her promise not to go to your *mamm*. I said it has to come from Ben. Oh, I don't know what they are playing at. I can't see it working, but they're just digging in deeper each day it goes on. Sure, I'm worried, but I feel utterly helpless here."

"I know," Emily replied. "I just hope it gets out soon, though I think it might start World War III around here at least."

"*Ya*. Maybe *Gott* can figure this one out," Phoebe concluded as she got up to go in to supper. *Only* Gott *can fix this one,* she thought to herself.

When she got home later that night, her parents were still up.

"*Kumm* in," her *dat* called to her as she slung her bookbag onto the back of a kitchen chair.

Phoebe sat down in the living room, wondering what was up.

"We heard that Gary passed away this morning," *Dat* began. "Jacob came by to tell us a little while ago. He said his family was around him and he went very peacefully in his sleep. Jacob said their whole family wanted to thank you for helping them get him home. I am glad you were able to do that for them."

"Oh, dear. Annie was so brave," Phoebe said as she dug into her pocket to get a tissue, which she dabbed her eyes with. "Such a sweet family."

Mamm added, "May he rest in peace. A lot will be *kumming* for the funeral. We'll start baking in the morning. Raisin Pie, I suppose. Funeral Pie. Have to have that. Then I'll think up something else to bring..." *Mamm's* voice drifted off as she thought about the next day.

The family sat together a while longer.

"I'll make us some cocoa, *ya?*" Phoebe offered.

"Sounds *gut,*" *Dat* agreed.

Saturday finally arrived and Leah was waiting for her ride into town. It was 6:00 a.m. when she headed down the long driveway to wait for the vehicle. Her girlfriend Naomi had agreed to pick her up in her car and drive Leah to her date.

Ben had just finished the barn chores with his *dat*.

"I'm going into town with a driver today, *Dat*," Ben informed him.

"I'd say this is getting pretty serious, son, eh?" his *dat* asked, though he was smiling.

"I'll let you know, okay?" Ben hastily replied, hoping to deflect any curiosity before he was ready to tell.

"Well, *ya* know I was in your place once, courtin' your *mamm*. You can talk to me anytime, *ya* know. I hope you will. This isn't always easy stuff, getting to know each other. Sometimes there are some pretty big issues, too. Don't stay away too long, okay?" his *dat* offered.

"Well, *Dat*," Ben began. *Gosh, is this the right moment? Should I spill the beans? I dunno what to do. I could tell Dat everything and that could be the beginning of the end. Maybe it's almost easier no one knowin'...*

"I should get ready and clean up, but can we talk tonight, maybe? That would be *gut*. My van will be here soon." Ben took a deep breath. "See, the thing is, she's Mennonite, *Dat*. We're trying to figure this one out. It's a pretty big deal. *Ya*, you and I can talk later."

Dat was silent for a long moment. Then he said, "Well, Ben, I see what you mean. Let's talk tonight. I'm glad you can tell me. I really am. We'll talk," *Dat* said as he patted Ben on the back. "You have a *gut* day," he added.

"What's her name?" *Dat* asked as Ben turned to go.

"Leah," he answered, barely whispering. "I love her, *Dat*," he said before he ran to the mud room off the main house and washed up quickly before he bolted along the drive down to the county road to look for the van. His father turned around and slowly made his way down the long barn. He had to think about this first, before he went in for breakfast. He couldn't talk to *Mamm* until he'd heard Ben out. *Shoot, I had no idea, Dat* thought to himself. *They sure picked trouble. Wow. Now what? Darn, I didn't see that one* kumming. *I wonder how they met.... He's pretty worked up about this, poor guy. I would be too. The bishops won't take to this kindly, I reckon. But*

Ben hasn't joined church yet; maybe there's a way. It's not like it's never been done before. It'll kill his mamm, *but ya know, there are worst things in life. He's a gut boy, just a bit, ah what is it? Clueless? Simple? Awkward? It's not like he wouldn't work hard and support a family. She couldn't be that far away. We could still see them, I suppose. Golly, what a pickle.* Gott, *please show me the way here. I could use some wisdom... really bad. Amen,* he concluded, taking a moment to look up at the sky as the dawn lit up the heavens above, then made his way up to the house.

Ben and Leah met in Rice Lake at the Wagon Wheel where she suggested they meet together. Leah had arrived first and was sipping coffee in a booth. She waved at him when she saw Ben come through the door.

"Did you have any trouble getting here?" Leah asked.

"No, the van was a little late; he had some other stops. How are you?" he asked as he reached across the table to take both of her hands in his.

"Fine. Good, actually. I talked to my mom," she announced. "She didn't blow up like I expected."

"Really? Wow. Really? What did she say?" Ben asked.

"She said we wouldn't be the first couple to have a 'mixed marriage,' she called it. I still don't see how two Christians who both want to live for God can be labeled like that, can you?" Leah asked, shaking her head.

The waitress came up to the table with a coffee cup and carafe. Ben nodded, and she poured him a mug, setting it down in front of him and placed two menus on the table before leaving.

Leah continued, "Well, each church gets pretty possessive about having 'The Truth' which discounts all the others, but no, I don't believe *Gott* thinks that way. You know that joke, where this man dies and gets to heaven and an angel is showing him around and when they get to a certain door, the angel signals him with his finger to his lips to be very quiet and tip toes by that door and then when he can talk again, the angel says, 'that's where the Catholics are. They think they're the only ones up here.'"

"No, I never heard that. It's a *gut* one. What else did she say?" Ben inquired hopefully.

"She said they had a couple in their church before they were married, some thirty years ago or so. He was Amish, and she was Mennonite. They got married and he became Mennonite and they had a big family. His family came to visit sometimes, too. I think my church might be a bit more forgiving than yours, you think?" Her raised eyebrows asking also.

"Maybe. I started to talk to my *dat* this morning in the barn. He didn't explode or anything. He might be more open to it than I figured. It's *Mamm* I am more worried about. I don't know if he can settle her down when she hears. She'll have a canary! It won't be pretty," he fretted, shaking his head and drumming his fingers on the table.

When the waitress returned, she topped off their coffees and took their orders.

"Would your *dat* be able to find work for me, though?" Ben asked.

"There are tons of jobs near where he works. There are the farms, the lumber mills, the construction companies, and stores: hardware, tree cutting businesses, roofing companies, it's a good area for work. I am sure he would help you," Leah said, hopefully.

"*Gut.* I guess it sounds better than it did yesterday," he added, but only slightly relieved.

After breakfast, they walked to Bear Creek hand-in-hand. They spent the morning walking along the shore, watching the fishermen pull in fish, one after another. They were catching walleye, sauger, northern pike, muskie, smallmouth bass, largemouth bass, channel catfish, flathead catfish, sturgeon, and all species of panfish.

"I never knew," Ben marveled. "We're gonna do some serious fishing here. I can't wait. Maybe we can fish next weekend, huh? Do you like fishing?"

"It's okay," Leah answered, chuckling. Fishing was not on her list of what constituted a date. "If you want to. I could bring a picnic basket."

"I'll bring my tackle next week if it's okay with you," Ben said, watching Leah's face to see if she meant it. She smiled and pulled him along toward the sandy beach at the end of the stretch where they were. It was deserted there. They could talk freely for as long as they wanted.

Sitting on a driftwood log, Leah began. "We could talk to our minister, I was thinking. Find out how long it would take, what all is involved. Then we could plan things. What do you think?" she asked.

"I could write to him, too, the minister. Can you give me a name and address? In your next letter?"

"That would be a start," Leah said. "And I can talk with my folks again. I'll let you know anything I find out there. I was thinking too, I know we pray at night, but the Bible says that 'where two or more are together, there He is in their midst.' What do you think about praying together whenever we see each other? Asking for guidance and for our families? Would you be comfortable with that?"

"Sure. We don't have prayers out loud at home, but I am *gut* with it. You'll have to teach me your church's ways. I don't really know anything about it," he spoke, feeling rather embarrassed.

"I could tell you some things or write about it. The important beliefs, you know," she began.

"Sure. Just so I don't sound like a complete dummy when I meet your parents or your minister," he offered.

"Well," she began, brushing her skirt back down over her knees where the wind had caught it. "We believe in the *Bann,* like you do, I think, where, if someone sins and won't listen to counsel and then refuses to listen to the church, they can be excommunicated or spend some time apart until they repent."

"We do the same. Shunning. It can be brutal. If it was me, I think I'd hurry up and mend my ways, maybe before it got that far."

"We call it shunning too, of the abomination, like association with the Catholic Church and other worldly groups and practices. Then we have the breaking of bread—communion—and believer's baptism. We have pastors and we're pacifists, not participating in wars or violence. That is pretty much what all Plain churches profess, I think," she concluded before continuing.

"There are several interpretations of all that, like the Old Mennonite Church, the Mennonite Brethren, Old Colony, Old Order, USA Mennonite, and the Mennonite Church of Canada. We also believe in going out and doing service projects which provide immediate and long-term responses to hurricanes, floods, and other disasters around the world. Some are okay with education past the eighth grade, and others aren't."

Ben was trying to take all that in. "It's not all that different from us at all. So why all the fuss? I just don't get it."

"I think it is nitpicking, actually. One theological point against another. And when they can't agree, they split off and start another group. I heard one group thought bonnet strings shouldn't be wide or showy and the other side disagreed pretty strongly and they split over that. How insane is that? The 'skinny strings group' against the 'fat strings group.' Do they ever stop and think what they must sound like?" Lean asked. "It isn't any smarter really than the Star-bellied Sneetches in Dr. Seuss's book!"

Ben started laughing. "That just reminded me—'fat strings and skinny strings.' When I was in school, we had a garden there. It was great. The teacher put a sign on the toolshed that said, 'lean wheelbarrows here' so they wouldn't collect the rain. Then some smart ass tacked another sign on the wall of the tool shed down aways that said, 'fat wheelbarrows here.' It took a while for some to get it," he laughed. Then, sobering up, he went back to their discussion.

"Well, we have groups in the Amish that were pretty upset when some started putting those orange slow-moving vehicle signs on the backs of their buggies so cars would see them better and there'd be less accidents, and some said the signs were too worldly, it was vanity, basically orange isn't allowed on buggies, and they split, too. Some pretty stubborn people out there with nothing better to do, if you ask me," Ben said.

"I know," Leah agreed. "But we also aim to not gossip, so we better not start pointing the finger now ourselves. We have a saying that goes something like this: 'Keep your words soft and sweet, in case you have to eat them.'"

"*Ya*, exactly," Ben agreed. "We have one that goes, 'If everyone swept before his own door first, the whole street would be clean.'"

"That's a good one. Ben, let's walk a bit. It's such a beautiful day," Leah suggested.

They walked until the sun began heading toward the horizon in earnest. Their rides would be meeting them soon back at the restaurant. Heading in that direction, they continued to talk, definitely feeling that the day had been constructive besides just fun being together.

"Oh, look. Let's get an ice cream, Ben," Leah asked as they neared the center of town.

"I can't believe I won't see you for 'nother whole week." Ben moaned, taking her hand. His was strong, and rough, yet gentle. She loved him so. Could one love even more than that, she wondered?

"We'll have to write, though it's not the same thing," she said.

"But we have work to do. Hopefully, we can get our folks on board soon. I just don't know about my *mamm* though. How *Dat* would ever fix that," Ben said, blowing out his breath and shaking his head. "And the ministers. I don't know. It would be easier to just elope."

"I don't want to do that, Ben. I'm really hoping there's a way so we can still be part of our families. I can't imagine you never seeing them again. Ever. That would be awful," she said, though clearly understanding his hesitation.

"I could never ask that of you. And I don't have it in me to hurt my folks like that. We'll be shown the way. I am sure of it," she said.

Their rides arrived shortly after and they waved goodbye after a quick kiss before the cars departed, until they became specks on the highways and disappeared out of view.

Chapter Ten

The Four Musketeers were meeting for lunch once again in the nurses' lounge at the hospital. Phoebe began the conversation.

"Leah, you seem happier today. Things going okay?" she ventured, though she would not have been surprised should Leah just get up and leave the table.

"They are," she replied as she unwrapped her sandwich, her eyes finally meeting Phoebe's after weeks of avoiding her. "We're both talking to our parents and the ministers, and things don't look so bad anymore. Maybe hopeful, you know? We still have a bunch of things to do, but it isn't like the end of the world anymore, with everyone forcing their two cents on us."

Susanna spoke next. "I don't think it will ever be easy for you two. There will always be people who won't agree, or just avoid you. We've actually had a few join us and then marry someone in the church later. Some think those are at a greater chance of leaving again, but I haven't seen that. They've mostly stayed committed, seeming to have found a real purpose for their lives. I think we should all be happy for them, even help them along, rather than hold grudges and make it harder."

Phoebe spoke up next. "My grandmother used to say, 'Our duty is not to see through one another but to see one another through.'"

"That's a good one," Leah agreed.

Hilda gulped her mouthful of coffee and added, "I have an uncle that married a college girl who came to us years ago. They have a big family now and you'd never guess she came from the world. Her family visits and has even attended church with us."

Then Phoebe remembered something. "We can't miss Susanna's wedding coming up next month. What can we bring?"

"Just yourselves. The *basels* will have it all arranged. Really," Susanna said.

"Does your community have a shower for you or anything?" Hilde wanted to know.

"The young people get together sometimes in the evenings and invite the couple. There's always gifts, mostly things we can use. One couple once got seven wicker laundry baskets filled with soaps and granola bars and huge bags of trail mix and those giant cans of caramel and cheesy popcorn balls. Each of our houses actually has a snack closet that comes with a key for all the candies and snacks, so the kids can't go in there. Twice a year our steward goes shopping in Minneapolis and divvies up all the goodies by weight per the number of people in the family, and the dads pick it up at night when the kids are asleep and lock it away," Susanna explained.

"That's some serious sugar addictions there," Hilde laughed. "You've got it down to a science! I'd hate to have to pay your dentist bills, gosh!"

"Like everything else, it seems," Phoebe added. "But I don't mean that sarcastically. It sounded like that, didn't it? Sorry. I just never heard of all the ways the Hutterites have figured out to live communally. It's fascinating, really." Phoebe continued, "Hey, you all, tonight Annie is having clinic again at her house. She organizes everyone who has asked to come with a medical question. It's fun, but it lasts all evening. She designates a waiting room and keeps people in order, first come first served, and sends them into the kitchen when the last person comes out. Any of you interested? You can stay over at our house and go in with my driver in the morning. You never know what people are going to ask. It's more about referring them to the right doctor or clinic in the end."

"Yeah, count me in," Susanna said. "I'll call home and let them know."

That evening Susanna and Phoebe arrived at the Gingerich's in time for supper. Annie was still running around setting up 'the clinic' as she called it. The kitchen would be fine the way it was and serve as an exam room, though Phoebe had assured her she wouldn't be examining anyone. Phoebe continued to tell Annie that she was hardly a doctor, and not even a real nurse, not yet. But most of the people she saw every Monday evening had questions, real questions that they had given some thought to and needed some answers for. Most didn't know where to go to see someone they could trust who wouldn't scalp them knowing they only paid in cash. They had avoided getting care, often waiting until an ailment became urgent. Or they had simply prayed and hoped it would go away but were still dealing with it weeks or months later. Preventative medicine had not become a concept in most settlements yet, further undermining the health of a whole segment of society, though not through any fault of their own. They had simply been written off by many in the medical community as uninterested, uneducated, or adverse to change of any kind, all unfounded assumptions. So, in the absence of sound advice from an advocate willing to spend time listening some had ignored the problem, chocking poor health up to fate, while others explored other options.

Rumor had it in the Plain communities in North America that Mexico, with its absence of a Food and Drug Administration and unregulated pharmaceuticals, held hope for some. Radon caves there, and their unscrupulous tour guides, promised cures from numerous maladies, including cancer. A whole network of drivers from around the U.S. and ending in Mexico had developed over the years while the Amish grapevine alerted people of the possibilities. Another 'cure' included peach pits eaten *en masse* when removed from the husk, also available south of the border.

Other enterprising Amish had researched the alternative vitamin and supplement market along with their claims of beneficial attributes and gone into business, making them available to their Amish neighbors from little shops set up in their homes. It has become quite a lucrative venture, actually helping some, but not all.

The living room was assigned the waiting room. Annie had a spiral binder already open on the big rolltop desk with all the patients listed along with their birthdates. She had taken it upon herself to organize Phoebe's visit. *She would have made an amazing corporate organizer—I am not kidding—in spite of her eighth-grade education,* Phoebe thought to herself.

"*Kumm, Mamm,*" Jacob begged. "You can do that after supper."

"*Ya,*" she called from the living room. "I'm *kumming.* Just want it all perfect."

"I'm sure it will be," Phoebe assured her, as Annie came to the table. Jacob brought the tureen of broccoli cheese soup to the table, carefully setting it down on a quilted mat. His sister brought a large platter piled high with soft pretzels and a dish of mustard. A large tea pot was already on the table with a sugar bowl and a pitcher of cream next to it.

Annie signaled for the silent grace ending with an audible 'Amen' and stood to serve the soup as everyone passed their bowls down the table. As she was ladling out the thick steaming soup, she introduced all the children for Susanna's benefit. "You've met Jacob," she nodded in his direction. "Next to him is Uri, then Rebecca, and Saloma. On this side is Caleb, Yohannes and Tamara. Seven kids."

"We've got a few *kumming* tonight," Annie informed Phoebe. "They should start arriving in about an hour."

When supper was over, Annie sat down and proceeded to read the list of appointments to the girls. Names and birthdates were meticulously handwritten in a beautiful script. No complaints or descriptions of why they wanted to be seen was entered, in compliance with HIPAA confidentiality.

After supper was cleaned up, sure enough, the buggies started rolling in. The first 'client' to come into the kitchen was a father with his eighteen-year-old son and the grandfather (who confessed, with a laugh, that he had come to check out the new nurse.) The father insisted that the boy must be sick because he had stopped growing. Susanna looked knowingly at Phoebe, who nodded her head ever so slightly. They were both thinking the same thing. This family could have been right out of *The Hobbit*—the grandfather especially, with his long white beard, felt hat, leather suspenders, and homemade linen shirt. They were all strong and sturdy, just very short men. Phoebe smiled and gave them their first course in genetics and dominant genes. She tried to reassure them, saying, "Junior is a fine specimen that you should be very proud of indeed."

Susanna suggested, "you might try to find a really tall girl for him to help mix up some of those genes, just not a first or second cousin, please." They were satisfied with the nurses' assessment, though disappointed there wasn't a pill that could fix him and make him instantly tall.

The next 'patients' were a mother and baby daughter who both were obviously affected by albinism. The mother wanted to know if all her children would inherit and pass on the trait or only a percentage of them, already quite sure they would because her own mother had it. Phoebe assured her she would track down someone working in genetics that could meet with them and give them some answers. The mother confided that she would try to avoid any more pregnancies if that were the case. As the mother left, Phoebe looked at Susanna. "She means that, *eh*? Not easy if you're Amish. I don't know what I'd do in her place."

"Me either," Susanna agreed. "Would a bishop ever agree to letting them use birth control in their case?"

"I doubt it," Phoebe said. "A real ethics puzzle. Yikes."

Phoebe later learned that there actually was ongoing research being done throughout the state, but because they didn't have a primary provider, they had never been referred to it. At least now they could speak to some experts and get up-to-date information to bring back home.

The next couple to come in were middle aged, with their son. He looked to be about seven, which surprised the nurses very much when they were told he was eleven. He was noticeably pale and thin. His parents weren't overly concerned. They just wanted Phoebe's opinion. They said they were still just waiting for him to outgrow it. Phoebe explained, "I am not at all sure what this could be, but you should have a proper assessment. We don't know how it might affect his future health, especially if left completely untreated, much less what damage it might have already caused." At that they said they were not interested in pursuing any further workups. They did explain that the child ate candy constantly. He had absolutely no taste for protein in any form. He had been catered to since he was a toddler. His mother coddled him and made anything he asked for, regardless of what was being served to the family that day.

Phoebe asked, "have you tried to sneak eggs into his daily waffles or pancakes that you make for him?" The mother said he didn't like them that way. Phoebe suggested testing him for diabetes, though he would have been in a coma long ago if that were his diagnosis. Finally, the father said they were not worried and felt that Phoebe was going overboard. He stood up to leave angrily saying, "As his father, I would know if he was truly sick— we'd be the first to know it!" After they left the kitchen, Susanna and Phoebe both shook their heads. Modern medicine had not, apparently, been accepted universally within the settlements. Both had naively assumed folks would be far more open in general. It was a toss-up. They would have their hands full in the coming years just educating people about their options, which didn't include burying their heads in the sand.

The next 'patients' were an older couple, both quite short and stout. The wife spoke for him. His brother had died unexpectedly the year before at forty-three of a massive heart attack, and she wanted to know if there was anything she could do to get this one into better shape. Susanna took his blood pressure, which was definitely too high. They had not been seeing a doctor regularly at all, so she explained that she thought that would be the first step. A doctor could monitor it over time and prescribe medications that should help. She also explained that diet and exercise were huge factors in health as we age. She said that they should first check in with a doctor and faithfully go to all his appointments. Then he spoke up, saying he exercises regularly at work all day long. Phoebe pointed out that walking, for example, will help his lungs and heart in other ways and aid in weight loss.

She gave them a brief overview of what foods he might need to think about avoiding but said he can also ask for a list when he goes in to see the doctor. Susanna suggested they walk as a couple for maybe an hour a day after their biggest meal, rather than going home to nap before the universal afternoon "snack" of more home-made pastries and coffee with fresh cream from the cow. Phoebe pointed out that their diet was high in meat and fats, fried foods and pastries, though they had an impressive amount of fruit and vegetables—both raw and cooked. Phoebe made a note to find a friendly G.P. in their area that she could connect them to.

The next 'patient' was a very sweet woman who knew she had a malignant brain tumor. She'd had surgery already and had opted not to continue any further treatments when it returned. She explained that she knew she would die soon but was grateful for every day she still had with her two small children and her husband. She was thirty-five. Both nurses were amazed at her faith and how very peaceful she was. She was not in pain at that point, and still had a reasonable amount of energy, so she was able to visit with her family still and was surrounded by a loving community. She knew her family would be cared for after she was gone. At one point Tillie removed her *kapp* and then her wig, (which both girls had not realized wasn't her real hairs) saying, "Look at this cute little wig they made for me at the hospital!" and with tears in her eyes she added, "I am so grateful!"

When Phoebe and Susanna saw her a few weeks later, she was still able to get around, though she stayed at home most days. They both wished they could do more for her. She would die at home the following August.

The last 'client' that evening was a young *mamm* with her newborn.

"Marvin is five weeks old. He's eating okay, but he's not gaining very well. My *mamm* says my milk is weak. My husband's *mamm* says I don't make enough and should get a pump and save it up and buy formula to supplement. My older *schweschder* who couldn't nurse says it runs in families and I've got to give up nursing. I'm so confused!" With that, she burst into tears.

Phoebe reached out and held the young mother's hand. "It isn't easy, especially with your first. Have you been back to a doctor, the baby's pediatrician, maybe?"

"Once, but they just said I should eat more."

"It actually takes eight-hundred calories *more* per day than when you were pregnant to make enough milk," Phoebe began. "If you are getting that, your milk should be adequate. You need to see someone who can follow you and help you through this. Most hospitals have a lactation consultant who might even be able to visit you at home and help make sure things improve. There is also a group of moms all over the world who help each other and have great advice and experience. They are called the La Leche League. I can see if I can find anyone in this area. You can contact them anytime you have a problem. They often meet at libraries or clinics and encourage each other. They found that they didn't have enough support and that many doctors didn't have any training at all in breastfeeding, so they grew out of that need. They started in 1969 and now are all over the world."

Susanna added, "I spoke to one doctor at the hospital when I was in labor and delivery training, who told me he had all of twenty minutes in eight years of med school on breastfeeding."

Phoebe continued. "One of the biggest obstacles to nursing is worry. And it sounds like with all the advice you've been getting that you are pretty discouraged. Let me see what I can get together and get to you in the next day or two, okay?"

The young *mamm* spoke next. "Thank you both so much. I really hope we can make this work. I was just about ready to give up, but I think you've given me some real hope. Thank you!" With that, she hugged them both goodbye.

Chapter Eleven

I t was a quiet *Samschdaag* morning. *Dat* had just left the table after breakfast, heading for the barn where the next set of chores awaited him. Stephen followed after gulping the last bit of coffee in his mug. Phoebe was savoring the fact that she didn't have to jump up and run to get to school or the next class.

"Any more coffee for you?" *Mamm* asked as she slid the thermos on the table down to her.

"No, is this your regular coffee? It smells funny to me," Phoebe said, scrunching up her nose.

"No, nothing different," *Mamm* replied. "Would you go and get the eggs for me this morning, but wait till Ivy comes up? She loves finding them, just like her *dat* did at that age. Did I tell you about the time he went out with his little basket to get the eggs and came back to the kitchen and demanded, stamping his little foot, 'I just want to know, was I born in the shell or out of the shell?'"

"Yes, you did, *Mamm.*" Phoebe answered, chuckling, getting up and heading for the *dawdi haus* door off the kitchen. "I'm just going to tidy up and maybe read a bit. I don't have a ton of homework, just a lot of reading this weekend. Tell Ivy to come and get me when she gets here."

Phoebe went into their bedroom and made the bed. She got out her textbook and lay down. *I'll just close my eyes for a minute,* she told herself, but was instantly asleep.

Ivy arrived shortly after, bounding into her *grossmammi's* kitchen and commenced to drag one of the chairs from the table over to the sink to help wash up the breakfast dishes.

"I'm turning fife, *Mammi.* Did you know?" the little chatterbox began.

"Yes, I do," her grandmother answered.

"Do you think I will get a cake? Will you come to our supper then? What will I be after fife?"

"Well, let me see. Yes, you will have a cake, and yes, *Doddy* and I will *kumm* down to your *haus,* and you'll have to wait a whole year for another birthday, but then you'll turn six," *Mamm* patiently answered. "What is your favorite cake?" *Mamm* asked.

"I like the one wiff the beets and chocolate in it, and I like the bwackbewy cake you make, and I like apple pudding cake, and I like cawwot cake and I like plum cake, too. Wiff ice cream, and icing. And candles. How many candles will I get this time?" the chatterbox asked.

"There will be five candles, unless we put on an extra one to grow on," *Mamm* answered, shaking her head.

"How do I gwow on a candle, huh *Mammi?*" she insisted.

"You don't, really. It's like, sort of like just *gut* luck, for the coming year," *Mamm* explained.

"Will you make my cake this year like you did for the others?" she inquired.

"Well, time will tell. Wait and see, dear," *Mamm* answered.

"And I wanna know, what does 'begat' mean *Mammi?*" she continued.

Flustered, *Mamm* turned, looking down at her and asked, "Where did you hear that?"

"*Dat* was weading the Bible at bweakfast to us and he said 'begat' but what is it?"

"Oh, it means they were born to someone," she explained.

"So my *mamm* and *dat* begat me?" she wanted to know.

"Well, I guess that's right. And I begat your Auntie Phoebe. Now you dry your hands off and go get her. She needs help getting the eggs for me," *Mamm* prodded, already exhausted from all the questions. "It just isn't fair they get all the energy and we're the ones that can use it," she muttered to herself.

"And I want *basketti* for supper on my birfday. Do you think *Mamm* will make it?" she continued as she climbed down from the chair and ran to the *dawdi haus*, without waiting for an answer to her last question. Finding Phoebe sound asleep, she ran back to the kitchen. "She's sweeping, *Mammi*. Should I wake her up?"

"Yes," she answered. *Why is she sleeping now? I wonder if she's getting sick*, she asked herself.

Ivy ran back to the *dawdi haus*, climbed onto the bed and jumped up and down while singing, "The wooster is cwowing...it's time to get up...it's your birfday today!"

Phoebe groaned and sat up. "Why, hi, there, little rooster. How are you?"

"We gotta get eggs for *Mammi*. Get up!" she demanded.

"Oh, alright," Phoebe said as she stretched her arms and legs.

"It's my birfday soon and *Mammi's* gonna make me a cake!" Ivy informed her aunt.

"Oh, is that so?" Phoebe asked as she dragged herself out of bed.

"Yeth," Ivy replied, jumping up and down once again. "Leth go!"

They walked back through the kitchen to the mud room to pick up the egg basket on their way to the *hinkelhaus*. It was a cool morning, but the damp grass felt good on their bare feet. The late fall was always Phoebe's favorite time of year, with the colored leaves, the morning mist, the wet grass, and the last of the wild berries. The last of the fruit was harvested, and the canning was winding down. Ivy skipped ahead toward the chickens, swinging the large basket, Phoebe taking up the rear. The chickens were already out of their coop pecking in the dirt along their fenced-in run.

"I just want to know," Ivy began once they were inside the *hinkelhaus*.

"I *need* to know, who puts the eggs under the chickens for me to find?" she puzzled.

Phoebe laughed out loud. "You're silly," she added.

"But *who?*" Ivy insisted.

"No one puts them there. You think we do all this just for your royal highness' enjoyment, do you?" Phoebe shook her head, incredulous at the inquisitive little mind.

"Well, how do they get there, then?" Ivy wanted to know.

"You really don't know?"

"Uh-uh," Ivy shook her head.

"Well, the chickens make eggs and lay them every day. Then we collect them to eat. *Gott* made them that way," Phoebe tried to explain as simply as possible. "And some of the eggs stay under the chickens and they hatch and become chicks."

"Oh, I see. So they begat chicks, right?"

"I guess so," Phoebe answered, totally bewildered now by Ivy's choice of words. *Where does this vocabulary come from?* she wondered. *Strange child.*

"Just don't bother the big black chicken over there. She'll likely peck you. She's sitting on her eggs so they will hatch. She doesn't know it's almost winter, and it'll be too cold for them out here and we'll have to put them in a box by the woodstove."

"And I can hold them then?" Ivy wondered.

"Yes, you can," Phoebe agreed. "Now carefully carry this back to *Mammi* while I shut the gate here."

Ivy skipped back to the farmhouse, humming another birthday song.

Chapter Twelve

"What are you cookin' for dinner, *Mammi?* Can I stay?" Ivy asked when she got back to the kitchen.

"Of course you can," *Mamm* said, bending down and hugging the little girl.

"Here, you can scrape the carrots for me," *Mamm* said as she handed Ivy the peeler and arranged the carrots on the sideboard. She wouldn't manage to do them perfectly, but *Mamm* didn't mind. She was just happy to have her grandchildren around her. Ivy finished dragging a chair over and climbed up on it, her little bare feet still covered with wet grass.

Phoebe came in and whispered to *Mamm*, "Remind me to tell you what someone said in the *hinkelhaus*. It's a *gut* one." Then she added, "I'm going to do a bit of wash today. It's sunny and I won't get time on Monday with school again and all."

"That's fine," *Mamm* replied. "We're just working on dinner here, aren't we, Ivy?" *Mamm* asked. The little girl nodded and positively beamed at the idea of really being needed and helping her *Mammi*.

Phoebe went into the *dawdi haus,* collected the wicker basket with the wash from the past week in it, and proceeded to the *weschkich*. She had put a large canning kettle of water on the cookstove after breakfast. It was boiling now, so she brought that in and dumped it into the large square galvanized washtub. Taking a measuring cup of powdered soap from a shelf above the washtub, she sprinkled that into the hot water. She took down a kitchen whisk that was hanging on a nail on the wall and swished the soap until it dissolved into bubbles before dumping in the laundry. She took up the dasher and began beating the clothes until she thought they were probably done. None of the clothes were really muddy or badly soiled. Stephen's work at the barn building furniture didn't leave any caked-on dirt like *Dat's* did after chores, though Phoebe had checked his denim trousers that he wore when he helped *Dat* with the cows. She unclamped the hose running from under the square tub into a drain in the floor as she squeezed each item and fed them through the hand-cranked rollers. From there, they dropped into the next square metal tub that was filled with cold water. After that, another turn through the rollers and a second rinse would finish the job. From there she'd carry the wicker basket out to the clotheslines.

"What's for dinner, *Mammi?*" Ivy wanted to know.

"*Frischi wascht,*" *Mamm* said. "Fresh sausage and noodle dinner, with carrots, cabbage, onions and sour cream all mixed in."

"And I'm making the cawwots, right?" Ivy asked.

"Yes, you are. *Denke,*" *Mamm* agreed. When she had finished peeling the carrots, as well as any five-year-old could manage, *Mamm* sent her out to help Phoebe hang the clothes.

"I made the cawwots," Ivy informed Phoebe as she turned around to let her aunt tie the clothespin apron onto her tiny waist. Ivy pulled out a clothespin from one of the pockets and held it up high for Phoebe to grab, all the while chattering nonstop about birthdays and carrots and chickens and eggs. The wash all hung finally, Phoebe untied the apron on Ivy and picked up the basket. "Let's see how else we can help your *mammi,* okay?" Ivy nodded, breaking into a skip on the way back to the house.

Reaching the kitchen, Phoebe asked, "*Mamm,* I could read until dinner if you're okay here."

"Sure," *Mamm* said. "We'll find plenty to do, won't we?" *Mamm* addressed Ivy, who was already nodding in agreement.

Phoebe lay back down on the bed. *I don't know what's wrong with me,* she thought as she soon drifted back to sleep once more.

Chapter Thirteen

Monday dawned crisp and cool. The fields had all been harvested. The root cellars were full. The colorful rows of filled glass canning jars sparkled on their shelves in the root cellar. There were still a few bushels of apples left over from the frolic waiting to be turned into dried *schnitz*. The cellar smelled sweet and the dirt floor felt cool on Phoebe's bare feet.

Choosing a pint of canned blueberries in syrup, Phoebe returned to the kitchen. *Mamm* was making oatmeal for breakfast. The table was ready, save for the blueberries, which Phoebe opened and stuck a tablespoon into the jar before setting it down next to the cream pitcher and a bowl of brown sugar. A canister of home-made granola sat next to that. The added crunch was extra good on oatmeal.

"*Mamm,* I'm gonna start before the others because my car will be here soon. I can't be late for class," Phoebe said.

"No problem," *Mamm* answered, beginning to ladle out a bowl for her.

"Just a little one for me, *Mamm,* half of that, *denke,*" Phoebe asked.

"How is Leah getting on?" *Mamm* inquired.

"Well, I thought it was hopeless, and for the longest time, she wouldn't discuss it with any of us, but she isn't such a space cookie now. Apparently, the Mennonites will take Ben and prepare him for baptism. Then they can actually get married. Her parents have warmed to the idea," she explained, adding, "somewhat."

"Well *his* parents haven't warmed to anything. His *mamm* is livid, spouting all sorts against him," *Mamm* informed her, "but to be fair, his *dat* isn't so stubborn. Ben never joined church here, so it's not like they'll shun him and he can even visit them, though his *mamm* is dead set against it all."

"Too bad," Phoebe answered.

"You've for sure changed your tune," *Mamm* said, turning away from the woodstove toward Phoebe.

"Well, stranger things have happened, I guess. They really seem to be convinced—that they are in love. 'Love at first sight.' I didn't think it was a real thing. It won't be easy for them, you know. But there are less suited couples out there, though. I really wish them happiness. It's just a mystery," Phoebe concluded.

"*Ya*," *Mamm* agreed. "Maybe his *mamm* will see sense. I hope she doesn't put her foot down and refuse to let them visit. That would be sad. It's not like he has killed someone or something. He hasn't committed a sin."

"I know. Emily told me she's trying to talk to her *mamm*. Maybe it is still so new. She worries what others will think of her, of them, Emily said. She can't be responsible for her grown son's decisions any longer," Phoebe said.

"No, but she still thinks of him as her little boy, I'm afraid. I hope she can see it in time," *Mamm* added. "Some do, and others never will."

"As if cutting your hairs and changing hats and the color of your shirt is such an offence against *Gott*. I can't imagine He cares one way or another, do you?" Phoebe asked.

"No, but it is not for us to say. The Amish have always upheld the traditions, and some think they are cast in stone and should never be challenged. Maybe the younger generation are more open-minded in today's world. I doubt they will ever convince people like Ben's *mamm*. They will die in their old ways, I am afraid. It has something to do with adhering to one's church and refusing to let doubt to come in; so instead they become staunch believers, ready to be martyred for the faith. Someone has to uphold the tradition and they think it is their calling to do it, otherwise the church will fall apart and scatter, I suppose," *Mamm* concluded.

"You're right, of course. I just hate to see it come to that, splitting a family that way. And they will blame Ben for it, not their own stubbornness. I wish life was more fair," Phoebe reflected.

"I know. It's really hard sometimes. But we only need to trust *Gott* then. His ways aren't our ways," *Mamm* said. "An old *mammi* once told me a story I will never forget. She said there was an *Englische* woman and an Amish woman; both had just died, and they were each on a ladder going up to heaven. It kept getting steeper and steeper and harder and harder to climb. The *Amische* woman thought to herself, *well surely I will get in, the life I've lived, and the modest clothes I've always worn, and my* kapp, *but that one, with her high heels and fancy dress and makeup and painted nails, well, I doubt it.* But it was the *Englische* woman who in fact got in first. The *Amische* woman had to wait. The other woman's heart was pure and humble, but the *Amische* woman had been proud and haughty. Gives a body something to think about."

"*Ya*, I won't forget that one either," Phoebe said thoughtfully. "Emily told me her *mamm* won't let her go to Ben's baptism or wedding. Not that she wasn't expecting that. She said you could cut the air with a knife over at their place. This isn't how it's meant to be."

Just then, the car could be heard crunching on the dirt driveway. Phoebe jumped up and took her dishes to the wash basin, and kissed *Mamm* on the cheek before grabbing her bookbag and running out the door.

Chapter Fourteen

T he Four Musketeers finally got together at lunchtime in the school cafeteria. "Coffee for everyone?" Susanna asked, getting up from the table.

"Not me," Phoebe begged out.

"But you are the coffee queen! What's up?" Susanna asked.

"I don't know. Just not in the mood," Phoebe said as she opened her brown bag, peered down into the contents there, and promptly closed it back up again.

"I'll be right back," she announced, getting up and heading to the deli counter. Grabbing a handful of saltines from the soup bar, she returned to the table. Carefully unwrapping one of the little bags, she nibbled at the corner of one of the crackers. "I'm just getting over some kind of bug," she said to the others.

"You have been looking a bit green around the edges lately," Hilde noted.

"I think it might be the nine-month bug, myself," Susanna offered with a sly look.

Leah looked up and gasped, putting both hands over her mouth, her eyes wide as saucers.

"Oh, I don't think so," Phoebe said, thought a moment, and then added, "Really?"

"Are you that daft *dindla*?" Susanna asked.

"No, I just don't think it could be that," Phoebe said, still bewildered at the thought.

"Should we buy you one of those tests that turns pink or blue or something?" Hilde offered.

"No, don't waste your money. They aren't always correct," Phoebe said.

"I don't think we need one of those," Susanna declared. "I have my answer there," she said, pointing to the saltines. The others laughed and whooped it up. Phoebe was pensive the entire lunch time. Heading back to class, she continued to be mesmerized by the possibility. *Really? Is it possible? I don't believe it. Already? It takes some couples months, even years, to.... Oh my! I sure hope I don't feel like this forever. I still have school till June. I haven't been able to eat all weekend. I barely got that oatmeal down this morning... Really? Well, that would explain....*

Mr. Schrock drove Phoebe to Annie's that afternoon after school for the weekly 'clinic.' Annie had supper ready and called the others to the table.

"*Patties* down?" the eldest son, Jacob, asked when everyone was assembled. He bowed his head, signaling the silent grace. After a minute he looked up and helped himself to a thick slice of fresh bread. His *mamm* passed him the butter dish. He took his new role as the man of the house seriously, since his *dat* had died so recently.

"Jacob, we aren't little kids anymore, *ya* know," Tamara informed him. "I'm already nine, for Pete's sake," she grumbled. "*Ya* don't have to say '*patties* down' anymore. Spare me!" she added, rolling her eyes.

"Okay, gotcha," Jacob laughed.

"So, how is school going?" Annie inquired.

"*Gut.* Oh, Annie, just a little of that for me, please," Phoebe asked as Annie dished up the steaming *rivvel* soup.

"Did you eat already?" Annie wanted to know.

"No, just a bit off today, sorry," Phoebe explained.

"When do you finish then?" Annie asked.

"We graduate in June. I still can't believe we'll be done. I hardly remember when I *wasn't* in school. Except I do remember when

Tamara was in my class, when I was still teaching. You were a first grader. Just a little bitty thing then, remember?" Phoebe asked.

"*Ya,*" Uri cut in, "and she thought that Shoo-fly pie was actually sh%&-fly pie because it was black and she wouldn't even taste it, and she thought that's why you had to shoo the flies away!"

"Not at the table, Uri," his *mamm* corrected sternly. "You know better! *Sham!*"

"Sorry, *Mamm,*" a slightly repentant Uri mumbled into his soup.

"I got to make the *rivvels* all by myself this time!" Tamara informed Phoebe.

"Really?" Phoebe marveled. "I only learned in my teens. *Gut* for you! Do you like cooking?"

"Oh, yes," Tammy answered. "And *Mamm* helped me make the dessert tonight, too. It's a surprise, so I can't tell *ya,*" Tammy whispered to Phoebe behind her hand.

"And I can't wait either," Phoebe assured her in confidence.

Tammy's eyebrows shot up. "Guess," she demanded.

"Should I? Well, let me think. Is it whoopie pies?" she asked.

Tammy shook her head, a huge sly grin on her face.

"Is it a cake?" Phoebe guessed. Tammy continued shaking her head.

"Is it pie?" Phoebe continued. Tammy was still shaking her head no.

"A pudding? Brownies? Cookies?" Phoebe guessed again. "Well, I give up. I will just have to finish this yummy soup and then see what it is." Tammy nodded a yes to that. "We'd better hurry and finish up supper before people start arriving to see Phoebe," Annie announced.

"Tammy, do you need help with dessert?" her *mamm* offered.

"Yes, please," the little girl asked. She and her *mamm* disappeared into the pantry and came out with a large pan of warm rhubarb cobbler and a gravy dish full of hot egg custard.

"*Ach!*" Phoebe exclaimed. "This is my favorite dessert. How did you know?"

"Well, um, we ah, just guessed, I guess," Tammy answered, quite unused to such praise. Both dishes were passed around until everyone was served. "Well, tuck in," Jacob announced, though still unused to his new standing in the family. "I'll get the tea," Annie said as she left the table to bring in the tea pot and milk pitcher. They all finished just as the first 'patients' arrived. The older children all pitched in to do the cleanup while Annie and Phoebe organized the visitors.

Part Three

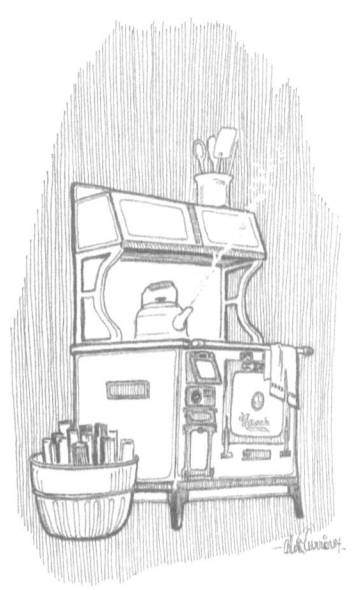

Chapter Fifteen

Mamm and Phoebe were enjoying a late morning cup of coffee together the following Saturday. Chores were done, breakfast had been cleaned up, and there was plenty of time before *Mamm* had to start dinner.

"I could sleep all day," Phoebe said as she stretched her arms out and yawned.

"Well, you are eating and sleeping for two, *ya* know," *Mamm* said.

"What? How did you know? I'm, uh, not even sure myself yet. I could just be late this month. There was a flu going around at school besides," Phoebe blurted out. "And I've been staying up late to finish all those papers for school. I could be just worn out, couldn't I? How—I mean, can you tell?"

"Yes, my love. It's written all over you, silly." *Mamm* had a way of quietly observing people. Phoebe had not been hard to read.

"So, you really think so? Really? When should I see the midwife then? Not for a while, I guess. Is there anything else I should know? It's all so new. Not like I have a bunch of older sisters telling me all this kind of stuff," she answered, totally flustered.

"*Ya*, it's early, but it wouldn't hurt to get to know the midwife and have your blood checked. Find out what vitamins you should be taking, things like that. Roberta has Saturday hours so you could go then," *Mamm* advised her.

"Oh, but *Mamm.* I want you to *kumm* with me. What if I forget something she says or wants me to do?" Phoebe was quiet for a minute. "You're really sure, aren't you?"

"You are going to be a *mamm.* Just think," *Mamm* told her, beaming.

"Does *Dat* know too?" Phoebe asked.

Mamm nodded. "It occurred to both of us the other day when you didn't want any coffee. That must have reminded him of me all those years ago. He hadn't forgotten all the little signs and such."

"Here you both knew, and Stephen and I didn't even have a clue. I've got to go and tell him," Phoebe said as she jumped up and headed toward the furniture barn. As she passed the outhouse, she realized that the last cup of tea was threatening to reappear and actually did the moment she got inside. *Well, my goodness. It's almost noon. Noon sickness then? Lunchtimes have been the worst all week. The saltines helped. But how can you gain any weight if you're sick half the time? I'll check out the school library first thing next week. Time to read up on having a baby. I still don't believe it.* Denke, Gott. *This has to be the most amazing gift of all. Please keep us healthy for the whole time.* Denke *for* Mamm *and* Dat *and Stephen, too. Amen. And it's okay if it isn't twins. We will cherish whatever you send us. Promise. Amen.*

Earlier that same morning, Ben and Leah had each scheduled a van to pick them up by eight o'clock. They met outside the same restaurant again, though this time they were both wearing their oldest chore clothes. Ben was balancing a fishing rod, a tackle box, two folding chairs, and a bait bucket as he paid the driver. Leah only had a large picnic hamper to contend with. She reached out and took the fishing rod as they headed off to the river.

"Hello, my darling," Ben opened up the conversation. "You are looking lovely today," he noted, leaning in to plant a gentle kiss on her cheek, upsetting the pile he was trying to negotiate, which sent half of it tumbling to the ground.

"We look like a pair of urchins, if you ask me," Leah said and then laughed out loud. "You don't look too bad yourself," she added.

Ben gulped hard. "Uh, well, what do you think? Not like these are my *gut* clothes. Your folks'll think you picked up some hobo, some 'knight of the road,' a real bum."

"What is that?" Leah asked him.

"A 'knight of the road?' That's just a nice name for a hobo, someone who rides the rails, finding work here or there, or camping out in the woods. There was one that came by our farm every summer for years when I was little. The only name we had for him was Bicycle Jack. He rode up to the farm on his bike every summer. He didn't have any teeth. He told us kids one time when *Mamm* and *Dat* couldn't hear him that he'd lost them because he used toothpaste, that it is the worst thing they ever invented, full of sugar. Then at supper that night *Mamm* made black-eyed peas and corn bread and he emptied the pitcher of maple syrup on his peas and mashed the cornbread into that—he couldn't chew real good because he didn't have any teeth—and *Mamm* told us later that he didn't have any teeth because he ate so much sugar and syrup."

"*Dat* would give him work. He'd sleep in the porch on a cot for the week he was with us and *Mamm* would bring him his meals. One year, *Dat* gave him the big sickle, and he cut down a whole field of scrub brush in a week. That time, he found a nest of bunnies and brought one to us. Its ear had been cut off when he was chopping at the prickers. I don't think the bunny made it, but I still remember him."

"It sounds like the gypsies that come by us each year. They work a bit too and leave a secret sign of some kind in chalk on the fence post by the road to let other gypsies know we are good people and will give them work and food. Did you eat breakfast?" Leah asked.

"*Ya.* I made a ham sandwich and coffee. *Mamm* and the little ones were all still asleep, and *Dat* and the boys were in the barn. *Dat* says to say hi to you. He wants to meet you," Ben said, watching Leah to gauge her reaction to that.

"*Ya*, that would be great. But your *Mamm*..." she trailed off the sentence.

"Nah. No change. She says I'm willful, and disobedient and selfish; at least once a day I get that. That I could have been perfectly happy with any *Amische* girl, but no, I had to forsake my family and church just to be an embarrassment to her. I am doing all this to her, *ya* see. It's so petty. I really don't get it. *Dat* is sad about it but can't do a whole lot. He says to be patient with her, that she might change in time, though I don't know how that could happen. It would take a miracle, but then *Gott* can do that, *eh?*"

"We'll pray together again before we go home this evening. I will also have my folks pray for her," Leah tried to console him. "So, when are you going to meet my parents? We can't put it off forever. Are you having second thoughts?"

"No, not at all. It's just hard to nail down drivers and all. Let's plan on next weekend. We'll make it work, *ya?*" Ben agreed, reaching out one arm around Leah's shoulder and pulling her close as they walked toward the river. She switched the picnic hamper to the other hand.

"Here, let me take that. You can carry the tackle box and bait. They aren't heavy," Ben insisted.

They were finally at the river and settled on a deserted section of the shore. It was a gorgeous day, not too cold when the sun came out, though there wouldn't be too many of those left before fall packed up for good and winter took over.

"This thing is heavy!" Ben complained as he hoisted the picnic basket up onto a large, flat rock. "What all is in here anyway?" he asked.

"You'll have to wait till lunch to find out," Leah answered coyly.

"Okay," Ben feigned disappointment, pouting. "Let's get those lures out."

They talked and fished for hours, completely forgetting the picnic lunch, if that were at all possible. There were plans to be made, parents to discuss, and dreams to be shared. Leah didn't mind holding Ben's fishy hand, either. She'd wash in the river, rubbing her hands with sand when it was time for lunch.

"I'm thinking it might be time for me to move out," Ben broached the subject he had been mulling over since he last saw Leah. "I am only irritating *Mamm* more by being there. She's miserable and mean, and I'm always defensive or hiding out somewhere to avoid her. Meals are the worst. Like the Cold War, with no one talking at all, just them sitting like statues or something. 'The Frozen Chosen,' I call them. I really feel badly, but I can't stand it. So unnatural, *ya* know? And she blames me for all of it. As if her attitude doesn't have any part in it. What about forgiving seventy-times-seven? Will she go to her grave like this? She even went so far as to tell *Dat* they should put a little table in the corner of the living room for me to eat at, as if I am already being shunned. Can you believe it? What do you think?" Ben asked, shaking his head.

"I agree it's time to cut the apron strings. I wish she could see you as a grown up and not some naughty, willful child. Maybe mothers are like that. No, I don't think they all are, but there are some. I'll ask my parents if there is a family that might give you a room. Dad said he's started looking for a job for you. He seems almost excited, happy. I've got to give it to them. They've really risen to the occasion," Leah concluded. "I was so afraid they wouldn't. Okay, next weekend."

"I'll be working at Miller's store all week. I am putting in some shelving there. You could call me, they have a phone. I'll give you the number. I'll be there by eight every morning," Ben explained. "Then we can nail down a few things this week, *eh*? I just want to move forward. It's been downright depressing at home. And the thing is, it really doesn't have to be that way, *ya* know?"

"It's *ferhoodled* for sure," Leah said, quietly looking down at the ground.

"What? When did you start learning *Pennsylfaanisch Deitsch?*" Ben asked and laughed out loud.

"Well, I thought it was about time," Leah said, smiling.

"*Ya* don't have to, *ya* know," Ben said.

"No, I want to. Then we'll be able communicate and the *kinner* won't know what we're saying," she added. "Like The Four Musketeers learning some sign language so we can 'talk' in class. Did you know that sign language is the only language you can speak with your mouth full? And the only language you can speak across the room without shouting? And underwater?" They both started laughing and couldn't stop. It had been so stressful all week, and this was the first time they could let off steam. And they were together. Would marriage be this much fun? Always? Could it be?

Chapter Sixteen

Ben and Leah were enjoying what would probably be their last fishing date. They had been hiring drivers to bring them from their homes to Rice Lake to meet every weekend. It was too far for Ben's horse and buggy to travel. Leah was still in the nursing program at the local community college, hoping to graduate in June.

Ben was ready to move to Leah's Mennonite community in another two weeks. Life at home in the Amish settlement had become unbearable. His *mamm* had decided that what Ben was doing was unforgivable, even though he had not joined church yet and would not come under the *Ordnung's* decree to shun disobedient members. He was exercising his free will and had fallen in love with Leah at first sight at the *youngie* singing back at the beginning of September. His cousin Phoebe Schwartz had brought three of her girlfriends from the LPN program for the weekend to experience Amish life. The Four Musketeers, as they'd called themselves —the four Plain girls at the college—had already spent time visiting Susanna's Hutterite colony and it was Phoebe's turn to host them. They got along famously, making school an absolute joy. They were all on schedule to graduate, despite the fact that almost twenty young women had dropped out of the two-year program since it began last year with over thirty students enrolling.

"So, my dear, what does your magic basket hold for lunch today?" Ben asked as the sun rose directly above them at noon. He walked down to the water and vigorously scrubbed his hands with sand, drying them on his denim overalls.

"You'll see, honey. *Kumm* up," she added in Pennsylvania Dutch, eager to learn for her husband-to-be.

Then Ben came out with a whole string of *Deitsch*: "*Kaanscht du muukka funge? Ich kaanscht won sie hucke believe, aver sie bleib net.*"

"And what is that supposed to mean, Mister?" Leah asked, rolling her eyes as she unpacked the picnic hamper.

"I said, 'can you catch flies? I can if they remain sitting, but they don't stay.' It's sort of like an Amish saying, something you say to show off, I think."

"Well, I doubt I will be able to rattle that one off anytime soon, I'm afraid," she replied.

"Mmmm. Looks great!" Ben said, surveying the contents of the blanket on the ground.

"Here, you can pour the coffee. There's cream in the little jar by the blue Tupperware there," she said as she finished assembling the dishes on the blanket. Ben just sat there marveling at his bride-to-be.

"Well *Dat*, can we say grace, please?" she said, showing off yet another *Amische* word she'd learned and proceeded to bow her head.

"Okay," Ben began, "*Patties* down?"

"What does that mean, anyway?" she asked, popping back up again from her pious pose.

"Well, *dats* always remind the *kinner* to take their hands off the table and fold them in their laps to pray. *Ya* know, patty-cake patty cake... *Patties*," Ben explained. "So we have started yet another family tradition, *eh*? *Patties* down?" he said smiling broadly at his bride-to-be.

They bowed their heads.

"So, what have we got today? It looks grand," he said after grace.

"Let's see. That is roll *kuchen,*" she pointed out, removing the checkered dish towel covering the bowl. "It's a dough that is twisted and then fried. You can dip them in the jam there. Some like it with ranch dressing. Those dumplings with the sour cream sauce are *vereniki,* a kind of *pierogi,* maybe Mennonite ravioli, I mean, sort of. Here's a serving spoon for that. And those are my mom's pickles, and some call this *strankel* soup, green bean soup, with ham and potato, in the thermos. I brought mugs for that. There's homemade cheese curds and that is *formavorscht,* home-made sausage. And we have apple fritters for dessert. We won't starve with this *fespa*—that's what we call a late snack."

"It looks more like a wedding feast!" Ben said, shaking his head.

"Oh, that will be very different, I promise. Trust me, you've never seen a spread like that," she replied, handing him a plate. They piled their plates up and ate and visited.

"Well," Ben finally said as they both finished, unable to take another bite. "I think the rain will hold off for us. Want to fish a bit more?"

"Sure. You start and I'll clean up everything here," she said, grabbing up the plates.

"Nope," Ben protested firmly. "In this family, everyone helps Mom after the meal. You did all the cooking, so we can at least do the cleanup and the dishes. Okay with you?"

"Um, yeah. Wow. Sure," Leah stuttered. "Fine by me, *Dat.*" She thought a moment to herself and then added, "But I don't think I want you to call me 'Mom.' I'm not your mom. I am going to be your *wife.* It sounds like bringing your mom into the bedroom, sort of, eh?"

"I agree." Ben answered, laughing as he bent down to kiss her.

They counted the fish they'd caught in the bucket and realized they'd reached the allowed number by four o'clock.

"We'll have enough time to clean up a bit at the petrol station before we get picked up," Leah pointed out.

"*Ya,* I must look pretty grungy by now. Not exactly how I

wanted to meet your folks," Ben worried as he packed up the tackle box.

"You are just your everyday self, not trying to impress anyone," Leah said. "They aren't looking for someone trying to impress them and being phony. I think you'll like them, and I'm sure they'll like you."

"*Gut* then," he concluded, though he still wondered if they might not like him and then the whole trip could turn mighty uncomfortable.

They had planned for Leah's dad to pick them up in the evening. Ben could meet the family that had offered him a room when he would move to the Mennonites, and he could spend time with Leah's family. His taxi home would meet him at her house later the next day.

Chapter Seventeen

Leah's dad walked up to them outside the restaurant.

"I didn't see the van," Leah said as she greeted him.

"Oh, I parked a-ways back there on the street. So is this the man I have been hearing so much about?" he asked turning toward Ben who reached out a hand to greet him. Leah's father gave him a big bear hug instead. Then he continued, "We've sure looked forward to this, Ben. You are one brave fellow. I don't know if I would have had the courage you have to see this through. I take my hat off to you, Mister," he added, thumping Ben on the back.

"Well, let's get in the car," Leah suggested. "It's been a long day, Dad."

They drove for over an hour out into the more rural reaches of the county.

"There's the Laura Ingalls Museum. See the log house over there? That's Pepin, Wisconsin. They were on their way to Walnut Grove after that and Spring Valley, too. Our claim to fame here," her dad explained.

At one point, Leah's father announced that they were now in Mennonite Territory.

"You can tell by the little road signs. Look, there's one on the right," he said as he slowed the vehicle down slightly. A framed wooden sign was mounted above a mailbox and printed in large letters read, THEREFORE NOW AMEND YOUR WAYS—

JEREMIAH 26:13. The next mailbox on the rural route had a similar sign that said, WHAT WILL YOU DO WITH JESUS? ACCEPT OR REJECT?... READ JOHN 14:6.

"Many of us use that as a way to minister to others. Like mission, though we go on mission too, where we can make the most difference. Some families change signs as often as once a month," Leah's dad explained. They drove on until they finally turned into a driveway where the sign there read, JESUS IS COMING! ARE YOU READY?... READ JOHN 14:3.

"This is us," he informed Ben. Just as they parked, Leah's mother came out of the house and heartily shook hands with Ben. "We're so glad you could come. This will be such fun, getting to know each other. Come in. Supper is ready."

"After that huge lunch, I'm not sure how much I can eat, though being out all day in that cold wind does give you an appetite," Ben remarked. He followed Leah to the bathroom, where they took turns washing up. He noticed the hallway and the living room as they passed them on their way to the bathroom. The house was noticeably brighter than most Amish homes, with the addition of electric lights, but it was just about as simple and free of superfluous knickknacks and framed pictures that *Englische* homes often boasted. The furniture was beautifully crafted oak and cherry he guessed. A lovely desk sat in one corner of the living room. A large calendar with a glossy photograph of a John Deere tractor hung above it, the walls otherwise unadorned.

Returning to the kitchen, they all sat down at the long table which was laden with dishes, some covered and others steaming.

Leah's mother was dressed in a long, light, green-colored floral calico dress with a matching cape-like panel over the bodice. *Definitely brighter than what Amish mamms wear at her age, but just as modest,* Ben thought to himself. Her *kapp* was also similar, but a bit abbreviated compared to his *mamm's* and his sisters.' Leah's father's denim trousers were a more modern cut than what most Amish men wore and his shirt was plaid, but he was pretty sure it was homemade, too. And it had a pocket, unlike many Amish shirts, which deliberately avoided them as (supposedly) contributing to vanity and materialism as you could fill a pocket with all sorts of extra stuff.

The kitchen was much brighter than the one he was used to at home, but other than that, not a whole lot appeared different. The curtains weren't the *Amische Ordnung*-ordered blue or green, but the rest of the room, with its tall hutch cupboard filled with glassware and expansive counter tops and pine cupboards, could have come out of any Amish home. True, the refrigerator here ran on electricity and his *mamm's* was kerosene-powered and their stove at home was hooked up to propane.

The supper fare was also similar in some ways and very different in others. Ben recognized the whole purple hard-boiled eggs pickled with beets, the bread-and-butter pickles, and the bowl of spiced applesauce. The other dishes evaded him completely. He would have to be introduced to those.

With everyone seated, hands were folded at table level, not '*patties* down' like he had been trained, and Leah's father began grace out loud, his rich voice definitely not subdued but heartily grateful for each member of the family as he named them, for their business, for the food, the animals, the rain for the crops, their health, and an earnest plea for all of them to become even more grateful and thankful and filled with faith. He thanked God for all of His blessings. He asked God to surround the missionaries who were away working for the Kingdom and he asked for healing for a neighbor and ended with a heartfelt plea that God shower Ben and Leah with His blessings and give them a long happy life together, rich in blessings and children. Then the 'Amen' ushered in a barrage of questions from the three little boys, who had been saving them up until they thought they would surely burst.

"Whoa there, fellas," their dad intervened. "We'll ask Ben about his family *after* we introduce ours, okay?" He paused a moment and then went on. "This is Nathan, our oldest, then Leah, then comes Yosef, Yacob and Simon in that order on that side of the table."

"I'm five," Simon announced.

Taking his cue from Simon, Yacob said, "I'm seven and Yosef is twelve."

"Thank you for that, boys. Now let's pass the dishes and eat before it gets cold," their dad said.

Leah's mother passed a large bowl to Ben saying, "these are cabbage rolls, and the next dish is *glums koki* which are cottage cheesecakes. I only make those for very special," she said as she winked at Ben. As the dishes were passed around, Leah or her mother introduced Ben to each delicacy. There was the special *paska* bread served with fresh butter and a zucchini casserole.

Leah noticed Ben piling on the food and leaned toward him to whisper, "Save room for dessert, please."

"This is all so *gut*. Thank you for this amazing welcome. I just wish my family was as open as yours is," Ben said, looking from Leah's mother to her dad.

"We're praying that peace will come into this marriage with your parents being reconciled there, too," her dad said.

"You are their only son, right?" Leah's mother asked. "That can't be easy for your mom. I can understand it'll take her longer. She's put a lot of stock in you taking over the farm for your dad and carrying on the traditions. This is not what she had ever imagined. You need to be patient with her, Ben. I know our prayers will be answered there, though I can't tell you when she'll come around, but I hope it won't be too long."

As they finished the wonderful meal, Leah's dad proposed they pray right there at the table for Ben's family. Spontaneous prayer was new to Ben, but it touched him deeply. So honest, so direct, so trusting that the Lord would hear them. Their lives were certainly dedicated to Him. That was very clear from the mailbox messages to the prayer when the Spirit moved one to pray.

"We can't forget dessert now," Mother said after the amen. "Maybe let's clean up and then have dessert after that."

"Good idea," her husband agreed, jumping up and heading for the rinsing side of the dish washing lineup while the children followed their mother's directions for carrying the dishes to the sink.

Chapter Eighteen

The Four Musketeers were back at school bright and early the following Monday morning. They would have to wait for lunchtime to catch each other up on any news. They were anxious to hear how Ben and Leah were getting on. They would also insist on an update on Phoebe's secret, which really wasn't a secret any longer, but neither was it being announced from the hilltops quite yet.

"Have you been to the doctor yet?" Susanna wanted to know when lunch time finally came around.

"No, but I did see the midwife on Saturday. I like her a lot. If everything remains low risk, I won't have to see an M.D. at all," she explained.

"But when is your due date?" Hilde asked.

"Time will tell," Phoebe coyly responded. "You know we *Amische* don't talk about such intimate things. That's the only answer you'll ever get from a *mamm*. But she is guessing in June. Gosh! I just realized I could miss graduation. *Ach!* Hopefully, it will be after that."

"Are you feeling better yet?" Leah asked.

"Much better. My *mamm* got me some crystalized ginger candy at the Co-op which works like a charm. She said she used it back then, too. I still can't abide coffee, but at least I can keep small meals down. I haven't started gaining weight, though, but there's plenty of time for that."

"Will you get an ultrasound?" Susanna asked.

"Not if everything is normal. If I suddenly start getting huge, Roberta said she would need one to rule out twins, things like that. Otherwise, no. She gave me a list of vitamins and supplements I should get and foods to avoid, like soda and processed chips. They're way too high in sodium. She's so sweet. Just like one of our own grandmothers, really."

"You'll probably have to make a bunch of new uniforms by January then. Yours won't fit anymore. Ugh, so much work," Leah said.

"Actually, our dress patterns allow for that. See the belt at the waist? That easily comes off and the extra panel in front can slide over, up to two feet and then be pinned or sewn back down. And the blouse has these three-inch side seams on both sides of the bodice which can be let out too. The shoulders don't have to be altered, just from the bust down. And the skirt hems are sewn double, so they can be let down and they are already hemmed there, too. Nifty, eh?"

"Very clever," Leah commented.

"Is Stephen excited?" Susanna asked then.

"He is so silly! I can't believe him," Phoebe laughed. "It's all he talks about when we are alone. The day after I told him, when I walked to the barn later to tell him supper was ready, he was tracing out a pattern for a rocking cradle onto some maple planks. He is funny. He told his parents, too. They are so excited, but I'm ready to talk about something else for a change."

Susanna asked then, "Did you know, in our colony, because everything is so communal and everyone talks about everyone else's business even though we are admonished not to gossip, but you know how *basels* are, most moms don't let anyone think they are even seeing a doctor or a midwife. They go through all these hoops to keep it a secret, to such a degree that some, but not all, don't gain any weight at all and surprise everyone when they come home with a baby. Prenatal care is sorely lacking because of it. I hope I can help there, maybe some education and then low birth weight babies will be a thing of the past. It is a concern."

"I'd say," Phoebe exclaimed. "That'll be quite a challenge. We also have a problem with prenatal care—some not getting any or just avoiding it, mainly because we don't have health insurance and it costs to go to the doctor or midwife. But if some issue gets overlooked, and the mom or baby needs extra care, that's mega-expensive, too, in the end. Kind of a Catch-22."

Lunch over, it was time to head back to class. The nursing program was definitely increasingly challenging. It was obvious that the students needed to cover the material required right up to the last minute before finals were upon them. They were also aware that the final research paper would be due before graduation, and they would be required to defend the material before an administrators' board. Their instructors made it clear that they would be available to help each student complete this requirement and suggested beginning with an outline. The afternoon class today would take the students through the process of writing such a project.

Finally, the last bell rang and the students all headed to the parking lot.

"What are you going to write about?" Susanna asked the others.

"I don't have a clue," Hilde moaned.

"Me either," Phoebe confessed.

Leah spoke next. "Maybe the ethics surrounding the right to withhold medical interventions on religious grounds. I did the ethics paper on it and I have a whole lot more material since then. I think that might fly, you think?"

"It's worth asking," Susanna said.

"We'd better get on it tonight so it doesn't come up all of a sudden," Phoebe warned them.

"Ya, I think we should know what we want to do it on real soon," Leah agreed.

"Okay, then, lunch tomorrow, we share what our topics will be?" Phoebe asked. They all agreed and headed for their rides home.

Chapter Nineteen

S upper had been over an hour ago and Phoebe was still leafing through her notes, trying to come up with a topic for her final project. She was sitting on their bed cross-legged in her muslin nightgown, her spiral notebooks spread out around her on the bear paws quilt. The gas lamp was casting shadows around the room as Stephen was getting ready for bed.

"I am thinking maybe I should write about the state of rural medical care in the Midwest. The statistics are staggering. Did you know there are less than thirty-nine physicians per 100,000 people in the Midwestern United States? That means that people in rural settings are gravely underserved, and their health is directly affected by that. Did you know that about twenty-five *percent* of rural children live in poverty? And that hospital closings have gotten to epidemic proportions... almost one a day, and that the number of obstetricians resigning is higher than any other specialty? Probably because they can no longer afford malpractice insurance. It is a disaster! Even though many states are completely paying off medical students' loans if they will agree to practice in rural areas for two years after they graduate? Two years only! That's crazy," Phoebe said.

"Sounds like a *gut* paper to me," Stephen agreed, hanging his clothes up on the wooden pegs lined up on the wall behind the door. Pulling up his pajama pants, he continued, "I didn't know it was that bad. We're lucky we have a midwife so close. I think the clinic at Annie's will prove to help out there, too."

"I just have to run it by my advisor tomorrow. I can also write about the Monday evening clinic and some of the things I've seen there. And I can interview some of our local people right here in the medical community. That would be *gut*, including some interviews," Phoebe concluded. "Real *gut*. I'm bushed. Time for bed, honey pie."

"What is a honey pie anyways? Is there even such a thing? Knowing your *mamm*, she'll invent one if there isn't. Look, I was up early with the cows," Stephen commented as he pulled the curtains shut. "Your *dat* has it down to a science, though. He's so organized."

Phoebe stacked up her notebooks and dropped the pile onto the floor over the edge of the bed where they fell with a loud thud. "I'll get them in the morning," she said as she yawned.

"Just don't forget they are there and fall all over them if you get up in the night," Stephen warned as he turned down the lamp until the wick flickered out.

"I won't," Phoebe said as she slid under the covers. "What do you think about Penelope?" she asked with her eyes closed.

"No way, at least if it's a boy," Stephen teased. Phoebe flung an arm over to his side of the bed, slapping him squarely in the chest.

"Pippa then?" she asked.

"What kind of a name is that?" he asked, shaking his head. "Sounds like a fancy little lap dog or something."

"Maybe Priscilla or Philomena?" she ventured again.

"Maybe we wait until we see what it looks like?" Stephen asked.

"It won't be an 'it' then, *ya* know. It will be either a little wood chopper or a little dish washer. We should have something in mind by then," she insisted.

Stephen laughed. "I heard of someone over at the Co-op— they couldn't decide what to name their new baby boy, so they called him 'Do-Dah' for three whole months and finally agreed on a name. In the end they called him Jesse. Can you believe that?"

"Poor little guy," Phoebe laughed. "I don't know what boy names I like. Do you have any?"

"Not really," he said as he rolled toward her. "Goodnight, my sweet," he said as he gently kissed her goodnight.

A minute later, she asked if he was asleep.

"Not now," came the reply.

"I don't think I ever told you the story about how we named our kittens one time when I was little. I couldn't have been more than three or four," Phoebe began.

"Okay, and..." Stephen encouraged her to continue as he rolled onto his back, his eyes still closed.

"We had this old cat that came with the house when *Dat* bought it. Well, we thought she was old. She was gray striped and skinny, but she sure kept the mice away. She would even run after the chipmunks and raid their nests. We called her *Schachdel*, old woman. Well, she got pregnant that fall, though we had never seen another cat for miles, but she had eight kittens. *Mamm* wouldn't let us hold them, though we could see them in a nest way in the back under the porch. Well, one night—they couldn't have been more than a week old—we heard this terrible racket outside and in the morning she was sitting there with two dead kittens and howling her heart out.

"Throughout the day, she located all of them where they'd been dragged around the woods and brought them all back to our porch, all very dead, almost like she thought *Mamm* could fix them. By that point, all of us *kinner* were howling, *Mamm* too. We had a proper burial in the flower bed, but *Schachdel* kept crying. *Mamm* said it was because she had so much milk and her babies were gone. We could only guess it was a raccoon, or a fox, or possum or something.

"Then *Mamm* had an idea. She got us all in the buggy and hitched up Alice and took off down the road. At the end of the road, maybe a fifteen-minute drive, she stopped in front of this house. It was more like a shack. She explained that an old widower lived there and was supposed to have bunches of cats, and maybe he could help us. She made us promise we'd stay put in the buggy as she tied Alice up to a tree by the road and went up to the door.

"This old *Englische* guy came out, and she explained what had happened. Then he offered to give her some newborn kittens so we could see if she would adopt them. *Mamm* came back to the buggy with a shoebox with four tiny kittens curled up there on an old rag. Two had their eyes open and two didn't. *Mamm* said he had bales of hay all over the house, in the living room and the bedrooms. She asked him how many cats he had and she said he guessed about thirty-something. So he went to a few of the nests of the new ones and got one out from each litter to make up the four in the box and told *Mamm* they wouldn't be missed. We put the box down on the floor of the buggy and us three kids sat there petting them as we drove home."

"When we got home, *Schachdel* was still sitting by the porch crying. *Mamm* sat down on the stoop and took her onto her lap. Then she told Abe to bring the box over. First, *Mamm* took out one of the kittens with its eyes still closed. *Schachdel* sniffed her and immediately started licking her. Then *Mamm* took out the next littlest one, and she started licking that one, too. She kept looking up at *Mamm* like she was saying thank you. It just broke your heart. Then *Mamm* brought out the last two, and *Schachdel* actually hissed at them, first one and then the other. We could only guess that they were too old with their eyes open already, so *Mamm* put them back in the box. Then we made a place in the porch where animals couldn't reach her this time with an old blanket and brought them in."

"*Schachdel* flopped down on her side and let *Mamm* put the two kittens by her, and they both started nursing right away. And that cat nursed those two for the next two years. They never got weaned. By then, they were both bigger than she was.

"*Mamm* got an eye dropper and dribbled warm cow milk into the two other kittens all evening and the next day brought them back to the old man. He was so happy she liked at least two, though, and he put the two kittens she'd rejected back in their nests. Of course, the next day it fell to the three of us *kinner* to name the two kittens.

"We sat in the porch and held them all day, so glad to have this happy ending. Abe wanted to name one Spot and another Rover. I said those were dogs' names. I wanted Cinderella and Little Red Riding Hood or Snow White, though neither of them was white. Isaac said those weren't real names, just make-believe. We must have gone through every name in our settlement. We suggested Rufus just as *Dat* was *kumming* in for dinner and he said that was disrespectful cause one of our bishops was named Rufus.

"After dinner, we went back to the porch and played with them all afternoon. I was holding the little calico one. *Mamm* said it was a girl and the other one was a boy. He was all black except for his white paws. Isaac was holding that one in his lap and had one of his front paws in each of his pudgy little hands. 'I know!' he said finally. 'His name is Little Fuzzy Fur Feet' and that's what we called him. That mama cat sure loved those two. *Dat* said he'd never seen anything like it."

"That is amazing," Stephen said. "But no child of ours will be called 'Little Fuzzy Fur Feet,' that's for sure," he chuckled.

"I named the calico kitten 'Orange-y' which the others approved of. *Schlaf gut,*" she said, then as an afterthought, "Maybe Stephen?"

"For a name? Nah. Then I'd always be 'Big Stephen' and he'd be 'Little Stephen' and I'd hate people calling him 'Junior' forever. No," he vetoed that one.

"*Mamm,*" Ben began. "I want you to meet Leah. I don't want this to come between us. You and *Dat* are too important to me to just cut you off." Ben held his breath then, waiting to see how this would turn out.

He had invited Leah for the following weekend, after he'd stayed with her family. He had prayed about how to go forward and not just run away and join the Mennonites without saying a word goodbye.

He had a hunch his parents wouldn't dream of him being brave enough to directly confront them like this, the farthest thing from their minds. It would for sure catch them off guard, but he also hoped it would be the most mature step he had ever taken, speaking to them as adults, not shying away from the biggest decision of his life. Certainly not apologizing and groveling like an insecure puppy, which was how he'd spent his first twenty-four years of life...

Chapter Twenty

His *mamm* was in the kitchen that Friday evening fixing supper. His *dat* had just come in from the last barn chores of the day and was washing up in the mudroom.

It was close to 6:00 p.m. when the hired car dropped Leah off at the end of the long driveway. Ben had arranged for a driver to pick Leah up after school and drive her to their Amish settlement.

His sister Emily had given Ben her room for Leah and offered to sleep on the couch herself. Ben had to let Emily in on his plans. He needed an ally, and someone to confirm that his ideas weren't too farfetched or *ferhoodled*. He'd barely slept the night before. Numerous possible scenarios played out in his anxious mind, some positively disastrous, ending with his mother ordering the couple out of the house and forbidding them from ever returning. He was banking on his *dat* taking his side and being the voice of reason here, maybe even laying down the law—the last word on the subject. His *dat* had that right, didn't he? Wives were instructed to be submissive to their husbands. She would have to be obedient. He hoped and prayed his *dat* would employ the age-old directive. Maybe his many prayers would be answered and his *mamm's* heart could be changed. *Mamm* was the last thorn in the whole equation. It didn't have to be this way, her way or the highway.

His *mamm* looked up from stirring the soup on the stove. Her eyes clearly registered shock. She froze in place, ladle held aloft. Ben's father stepped up to Leah and shook hands with her.

"I'm real glad you've *kumm,*" he said, forcing his eyes to stay on Leah and not give in to checking *Mamm* out quite yet. Ben's older sister Emily had quietly slipped into the kitchen and greeted Leah next. Then their dad invited everyone to sit down at the table.

Emily ran to get another table setting, which she brought and set down.

"*Mamm,*" Ben's dad began. "*Kumm sits ana,* dear."

"Did you know about this?" she demanded, facing *Dat.* "You're all in on it, are *ya?*" she asked, raising her voice and angrily scanning all the faces at the table.

"No, I didn't know. Here, *kumm* sit by me. We can at least hear him out. Ben obviously has something to say to us," *Dat* urged her.

Grabbing the corner of her apron, she began twisting it as she sat down, her frowning eyebrows still registering her fury and rage.

"Um," Ben began. "*Mamm, Dat,* I don't want to just up and leave my family."

"No, you just want your cake and to eat it, too!" she stormed at him.

"*Mamm!*" *Dat* said firmly. "We are going to hear him out now, and we aren't going to say anything at all till he's done. I mean it." Then *Dat* nodded at Ben to continue.

"I want you to know that I am not marrying Leah to spite you. *Gott* brought us together and I thank Him every day for that. Our deepest wish is that you will give us your support and keep us in your prayers. Maybe even your blessing."

"What will people think? What will they say? 'Oh those are the people whose son ran off and married outside,'" his *mamm* practically yelled.

His *dat* cut in at that point, speaking more forcefully than he had yet. "Look," he began. "No one has died. No one is being unfaithful to their baptism vows. Our kids aren't on drugs or in jail, like some, and frankly, I don't care what people *think!* They can ask me what *I* think. I think we've raised a loving, kind, obedient son. It's about time he writes his own declaration of independence.

From now on, he and his new family will be welcome in my house. Does everyone understand that?"

"So now it doesn't matter what I think anymore?" *Mamm* turned on him, hate in her eyes.

Dat took a deep breath and began, "The Gospel tells us what to think, how many times to forgive, how to be kind to one another, tender-hearted, forgiving each other, just as God in Christ also has forgiven you." *Dat* got up at that point and taking long strides across the kitchen in his stockinged feet, went and brought back his Bible from the table by his rocker in the living room. Opening it up, he quickly found what he was looking for.

"Here it is," he said, sitting back down. "'Therefore, ye be imitators of God, as beloved children, and walk in love, just as Christ also loved you, and gave Himself up for us, an offering and a sacrifice to God.'" *Dat* closed the book then. "This is what our whole lives have taught us and we can finally put it into practice, *ya?*" he asked, looking around the table. "And I found this a while ago and stuck it in here 'cause I liked it," he went on, opening up the back cover. "Here it is, by Thomas Watson, who was a Puritan preacher in the sixteen-hundreds. He writes, 'Resist revenge, do not return evil for evil, wishing them well instead and grieving at their calamities, praying for their welfare, seeking reconciliation so far as it depends on you, and coming to their aid in distress.'" He paused to let that sink in. Then closing the Bible, he boldly declared, "Now, I say this is what this family will live by from now on, and if we can't then we have no business calling ourselves Christians." He had spoken.

The kitchen went silent. *Mamm* was looking at her hands in her lap, tears running down her cheeks.

Then *Dat* said firmly, "Let's say grace, then, eh?" and bowed his head.

Chapter Twenty-One

Susanna's wedding would be the next event among The Four Musketeers. It was planned for the first Sunday in November. Not only were Susanna's fellow Musketeers and their significant others invited, but everyone from the surrounding district: English neighbors, farm vendors, and relatives and friends from near and far Hutterian colonies. Baking for the celebration had begun weeks in advance. The wedding cake had been made and the five layers frozen but not decorated yet. The school children were busy making posters to decorate the dining room walls.

Susanna's family need not worry about the preparations. The entire community would take care of everything. Susanna's mother was busy sewing a new dress for her. Though some brides wanted a white wedding dress, made from the same pattern as the girl's everyday *tract,* though with a few embellishments, there was no practical way to use it again after the special day. Susanna also pointed out that she had been wearing white on all the clinical days she'd attended school for the past year and a half and didn't want to look like a nurse on her wedding day too, so she chose instead a light floral patterned teal fabric that would become her Sunday best after the wedding.

"Mudder," Susanna began, as she sat next to her mother in the tiny sewing room in their apartment. "How do I know I don't need

to do anything for our new place? Have you checked yet? I mean, like dishes, linens, lamps, all that?"

Her mother was busy sewing on her dependable Pfaff machine. Sewing machines were one of the few possessions that Hutterite women were not required to share communally. Since they were each responsible for making their family's clothes, each sister was gifted with one when she married. Her mother stopped sewing and looked up. "You don't have to worry about it. Yes, it is all there. It's perfect. We'll just bring over your clothes from here the day before. Nothing at all to fret over."

Susanna and Levi were not allowed to see their new apartment yet. It was a secret. Her sisters and girlfriends would have the honor of fixing it up. They would place each gift and accompanying card in the new place. The windows would have new homemade floral curtains. The table there would be covered with flowers and cards as well as every dresser and bookcase top. There would be chocolates and candy sprinkled on the bed, which would be boasting a brand-new handmade quilt, and matching pillow shams.

The kitchen counters would be covered with handmade cutting boards, new dishes and glassware and fruit baskets; even handmade, quilted hot pads.

The shower would have a new handmade shower curtain, a basket of fancy soaps and lotions, and monogrammed towels. No detail would be missed. The candy closet would be well stocked as well as the snack cupboard where the new couple would find everything from mixed nuts to cheesy popcorn, store-bought cookies, pretzels, assorted crackers, Nutella and peanut butter.

There would even be a games shelf in one of the closets with a new Monopoly game, Scrabble, Boggle, Dominoes, Uno, Chinese Checkers, Rummikub, and other card and board games that become essential—actually vital—come long winter evenings.

There are no TVs on Hutterite 'hofs, no radios, computers, smart phones, etc., so homemade entertainment is raised to a whole new level here. Another shelf would hold boxes of brand-new puzzles that can be traded for other families' puzzles once completed and taken apart again. There might even be a toy box on wheels under the handmade living room sofa, ready with an assortment of homemade dolls, miniature John Deere tractors and some tiny Hot Wheels for any little people who might be visiting and need a distraction.

Susanna was hardly aware of all the activity behind the scenes as she spent every waking moment at home doing homework, keeping her uniforms washed and ready, and attending daily prayer services. She often snuck into the communal kitchen, carefully avoiding the communal dining hall, quickly scooping up her dinner or supper into little metal pails and left by the kitchen's back door to bring home and eat while she studied.

In the evenings, Levi would come by her house and visit with the family in the living room. Occasionally, he would wander down to Susanna's room and quietly tap on the door.

"Come in. I know who you are," she would tease. He would enter and stretch out on one of the beds, his hands folded behind his head.

"Wait until I finish writing this paragraph..." Susanna requested, without taking her eyes off her place on the page.

"There, done," she said.

"So, what's new?" Levi began.

"Oh, you know. School, school and more school. I can't imagine what it'll be like when I'm done. I can't remember back to when I wasn't in school," she moaned.

She got up and sat by him on the bed. "How are you? Anything new?"

"No. Same old same old, *ya* know. Oh, my dad said I can stay on at the hog barns for now. There'll always be work. The work distributor will see to that," he answered.

"Did I ever tell you what we used to call the *basels'* work distributor? We called her 'the work disturber.' I'm sure she knew that, but she never let on. *Ya* know, we should do something fun this weekend. Can you request a car?" she asked.

"*Yo*. What do you wanna do?" he inquired.

"Oh, run away and elope to Mexico, maybe," she laughed. "No, honestly, let's think up something fun. We could go visit Phoebe and surprise them? She said we should come by anytime. You've never been to an Amish farm, have you?"

"No. That would be fun. We could leave early on Saturday. Maybe ask your *mudder* for some fresh sausage and Danish or something to bring them from our stores," he suggested.

"Oh, yes! I can't wait. I just have to do something else—*anything* —just to break up the monotony. Will she ever be surprised," Susanna noted.

Levi continued, "Make us a thermos of coffee and some sandwiches for breakfast on the way. We can leave by six then. They're only two and a half hours away, right?"

"*Yo.* Oh! I haven't told you what I've been knitting while I'm in the van coming and going to school," she said as she jumped up and took out a knitting bag from her top drawer. "Here it is. I just finished them. I can bring them along too, all wrapped up." She held up two adorable little yellow knitted baby booties.

"Are those big enough for a baby? They look like they're for a doll," he complained.

"No, they are just right, silly. Babies come pretty little if you haven't noticed," she chuckled.

"I know that, but they're so small. They're cute, though," he admitted.

"I've started a little sweater to match, too," she added. "And a hat."

"I can't imagine what it's like to have your own, though," Levi pondered.

"I know. It's different when it's one of your older brothers' or sisters' babies, but your own... I can't imagine," she mused.

"Let's not get too excited yet, okay? Some don't get pregnant right away. We'll just wait and see, eh?" he advised.

"I really can't get too excited with school and all. My head is so full right now, thinking of finals week. That'll be here before we know it. And the research paper before that. Ugh. Too much to think about," she sighed.

"Okay, then," Levi said as he sat up. "Tomorrow is Friday and then Saturday and we'll go visit your friend. It's supposed to be sunny all weekend. We can go by that farmer's market on the way, the one off Highway 94. You haven't been there this year at all, have you?"

"No, I haven't. This is getting better and better. Thank you!" she said as she planted a kiss lightly on his cheek.

"No, you won't get away with just that. Come here," he said as he wrapped her in his arms and gave her a proper kiss.

"But that's all, mind you," she admonished him, pulling away. "For now." She laughed.

Chapter Twenty-Two

Hilde's parents had laid down the law and insisted she wait until after she graduated from the nursing program to date at all. It was easy to agree to that when it was all so new and she was feeling overwhelmed by the homework at the beginning. But it was now the second half of the course, one year already in the past and less than one year to go.

She had developed a regular routine for doing her assignments, the required reading, writing papers and going to the clinical days at the hospital. She had recently allowed herself a few diversions since this second year had begun. Almost every evening, a group of the young people from the neighborhood would get together when the weather was nice and play volleyball. When it was raining or too cold, the activities moved inside, and board games would be accompanied by hot cocoa and snacks.

On weekends, larger gatherings were held, often taking place in a barn where the young people could sing together. Dancing wasn't permitted by the Mennonite *Ordnung*, but it wasn't exactly forbidden either. Some of the more progressive churches allowed traditional folk dances. At one of these get-togethers, Leah and Hilde had gone together and were sitting visiting.

"I say we don't talk about school or our term papers this evening," Leah suggested.

"Good idea. I am so glad for a night off. Can you imagine school being over for good?" Hilde asked.

"Nope. I can't wait, but we're not talking about that tonight, remember?" Leah answered just as someone put a cassette tape into a player and an old German circle dance began. Boys and girls scurried to find partners.

"Is Ben here this weekend?" Hilde asked Leah.

"No, they're doing a big wood project this weekend, like a *frolic*, getting wood split and piled up for all the older people at their homes around the settlement," she explained. "He's coming to live by us in a week, though. There's a family that offered him a room and he's taking instructions for baptism by Christmas. Then we can set a date. I really never thought this could work. It's a miracle, really."

"You mean his family is okay with it now?" Hilde asked, surprise obvious in her raised eyebrows.

"Absolutely. I said it was like a miracle. I am so grateful. We can actually talk to his folks. His *dat* really laid down the law and told it like it is and she had to agree. His mom is slowly warming up to the idea, but we're trying to give her some space," Leah explained.

"That's really wonderful," Hilda answered just as a young man walked up to her and offered his hand.

"May I have this dance?" he inquired, bowing slightly.

"Um, o-kay..." Hilde answered, looking at Leah and then back at the handsome fellow, as she blushed for all to see.

She stood up and took his hand as he led her to join the large circle with him.

"I don't really know how to dance," she began.

"That's okay," he replied. "Most of us don't. We're just learning." He laughed. "Hang on," he warned her. "This is a fast one," he said as the circle began moving to the left.

"I'm Hilde," she spoke over the music.

"Hi. I'm Ivan. We're visiting our cousins here from Indiana. Do you live here?" he asked.

"Yes," she replied.

"I was here with my cousins last week, but I didn't see you then," he commented.

"No, I just started coming again. I'm in college just now and had a ton of homework last week," she explained.

"Really?" he asked as the music was turned up another level. "Let's visit after this, okay?" he loudly suggested.

Hilde nodded as she tripped over one of her feet, the circle picking up speed along with the music. Ivan caught her arm, and she quickly recovered, falling back into place as the circle reversed directions. Then the entire circle stepped toward the center, and as they all held hands, raised them and then stepped back once more to resume dancing clockwise. Finally, the music slowed down and then stopped.

"Whew, that was intense," Hilde observed, catching her breath.

"I like that one. Let's visit over here," Ivan suggested. "Can I get you some punch?"

"Yes, I'd like that," she agreed, watching him walk away. *Huh,* she thought. *He's cute...handsome, I'd say. Where did he say he was from? Why me? With all these girls here. Well, this is a surprise. Can't tell the folks, though. Not till I graduate. Well, here he comes. Yes, he'd be a keeper, I think. Definitely up there in the running. Gosh. Golly.*

He came back shortly with two tall glasses of punch. "Tell me about college," he began. "I don't know of any girls who go on with their education; maybe some boys doing agriculture or welding and such."

"The community decided to send some girls to become LPN nurses so we can help out more at home with mothers and older people. It's been really interesting, a whole 'nother world, actually," she explained. "There are four of us Plain girls in the program, which makes it super fun. We'll graduate this coming June. It's plenty of work and I'll be glad when it's over," she said as she sipped the cold drink. "Leah, the girl I was sitting with before, is in school with me."

"Yeah, I know her family," Ivan said. "Isn't she the one that hopes to marry the Amish fellow?"

"Yes, that's her. I think it is actually going to happen. I am happy for them," she said.

"Wow. I can't imagine," he pondered, shaking his head. "That can't be easy."

Hilde and Ivan sat out the next few dances, preferring instead to talk and get to know one another. The final last dance ended and the young people descended on the snack tables for the last time before heading home.

"I'd like you see you again, if you'd like to, too," Ivan said. "Can I give you my phone number? We can stay in touch?"

"Sure," Hilde answered, blushing again, so surprised at this turn of events. Ivan pulled a pencil and a tiny appointment book out of his pocket and quickly scribbled his phone number before tearing the page out and handing it to her.

"Thank you. That was such fun," she said as the crowd pulled them apart, each one going in a different direction. The last she saw of Ivan that night was a glimpse of him waving goodbye over the heads of the other young people. He'd been grinning from ear to ear and waving.

Leah caught up with Hilde as they found the car they'd come in with two friends from the same part of the district.

"So, who was that?" Leah asked as she and Hilde tumbled into the back seat.

"His name is Ivan," Hilde answered, still bewildered but also delighted by the encounter.

"Is he nice?" Leah pried.

"Oh, very. We hit it off right from the beginning. He's visiting here from Indiana," she explained.

"Are you going to see him again?" Leah continued.

"I think so," Hilde replied.

"What do you mean 'you think so?'" Leah insisted.

"I have his phone number. I guess it would be fun to get together again. I'll have to wait till I'm caught up with my homework first. I gave up a whole evening writing that paper tonight. I'll call him after that, hopefully," Hilde planned.

"Is it love at first sight? Hmm?" Leah persisted.

"Not exactly, but he's ever so sweet. Cute. Very tall. I can't guess how old he is. Obviously single," Hilde giggled, realizing how very little she knew about him.

"You didn't ask him?" Leah berated her.

"No, we didn't have a lot of time. The evening was over so fast," she apologized.

"What does he do? Who are his relatives here? How long will he be here?" Leah demanded.

"I don't know!" Hilde said, becoming quite overwhelmed by the barrage coming from Leah. "I don't know. That's why we want to get to know each other. Now don't ask me anymore questions."

"I'm sorry," Leah backed off. "I am just so happy for you. Sorry."

"Okay," Hilde answered. Then, smiling shyly and blushing once again, she added, "Stay tuned. Time will tell."

Chapter Twenty-Three

Phoebe sat at the kitchen table enjoying a rare coffee break with her *mamm*.

"I can't remember the last time having coffee with you all by ourselves! It's nice. We should do this more often, eh?" Phoebe said. "Anyone *kumming* to dinner today or tomorrow? It's a no-preaching Sunday, right?" Her *mamm* bobbed her head while swallowing her coffee.

She cleared her throat and answered. "No, no visitors that I know of. I'm glad, too, I have to admit. This mental pause stuff wears me out lately."

"Mamm," Phoebe said, taking a deep breath. "It's men-O-pause," she carefully enunciated. "You went to see the doctor didn't you? What did she say?"

"Oh, she gave me these pills for my blood pressure and said she could give me some hormone supplements but that it was better if I could just weather it without all that. I have to go back in two weeks. I said okay," *Mamm* reported. "Millie, over in the next district, swears by evening primrose oil and black cohosh tea. I might try that too," *Mamm* mused.

"And here you're on your third or fourth cup of coffee today? All the pills and natural remedies in the world won't do a thing if you don't change your diet. Didn't she say anything about that? About coffee? Salt?" Phoebe asked.

"*Ach, ya.* But you can't just change your whole life around in a day," she complained.

"Well, yes, you can. We'll get some decaffeinated coffee for you. *Grossmammi* had to switch, remember? You'll feel so much better when we get it under control. I promise. And let's not cook with any salt anymore, either. None at all. Just use what's on the table or a substitute like Dash or Braggs. You can get used to anything, you'll see," Phoebe encouraged her. "And I get to keep you around for another twenty or thirty years then, eh?"

"Don't wish that on me," her *mamm* groaned.

"You're just feeling poorly today. Just think of all the grandbabies you are going to have to rock for me," Phoebe laughed.

"Let's just get this one out and healthy first," *Mamm* replied, perking up slightly. "That reminds me of one of my *Mamm's* old sayings, your *grossmammi's*: 'A mother is a gardener of *Gott* tending to the hearts of her children.' Gosh, if folks knew ahead how much work it all would be, I don't know if anyone would ever have *kinner.*"

"That's why we don't know. I think it's also why they're so cute, so we'll long to have them, over and over, eh?" Phoebe said, pouring herself another cup of coffee.

"*Mamm,* did you know our baby is the size of a grape?" Phoebe asked.

"How do you know that?" *Mamm* looked at her, completely flummoxed, evidenced by her frowning eyebrows.

"Well, I'm about nine weeks along. We have these charts at school that tell you how big your baby is each week. Last week he was the size of a kidney bean and the week before that he was as big as a blueberry. And in two weeks, he'll be as big as a fig. Isn't that amazing?" she marveled. "And moms can even get it sent to their phone each week automatically. We're doing a chapter on patient education—educating people about their health so they can participate in their own care. It is amazing how many people neglect it completely and the damage it causes is enormous."

"Hmm," *Mamm* was still thinking about a baby being the size of a grape. "So when can they tell if it's a girl or a boy?"

"The earliest is about eighteen weeks when it's the size of a green pepper, but they can only detect it through ultrasound at that point. I don't think I want to know. I want it to be a surprise. So does Stephen."

"How are Leah and Ben doing?" *Mamm* asked absentmindedly.

"They're *gut,*" Phoebe replied. "She's not the space cookie I thought she was. They're definitely finding their way. Keep them in your prayers, *eh?*"

Mamm nodded silently and then sat quietly, sipping her coffee, taking all of this new information in. She startled when someone loudly banged on the back door. Phoebe popped up to see who it was. She flung open the door, genuinely surprised to see Susanna with her young man along.

"Oh my goodness," she squeaked. "You came!"

"You told us to drop by anytime," Susanna explained as she hugged Phoebe. "I just needed to get out of the house today," she explained. "This is Levi," she introduced him.

"This is such fun, *eh?* Can you stay all day?" Phoebe wanted to know.

"Sure, unless you're busy," Susanna replied.

"No, nothing on. I can show you around the district, and we can come back and help *Mamm* with dinner. Stephen and *Dat* will be back by then, but no one else that we know of. Oh, I am so glad you came," Phoebe said as she squeezed Susanna's hand. Then Susanna took the brown bag of homemade bakery goods from Levi and handed it to Phoebe saying, "Just some goodies to enjoy from home."

"Oh, thank you so much," Phoebe replied.

"*Mamm,* can we take the buggy? It should only take us an hour and we'll *kumm* back and help you," Phoebe asked.

"*Ya,* for sure. See you soon. Have fun," *Mamm* said.

"This is for you, too," Susanna said as she handed Phoebe a little wrapped box, topped with a bow. "Open it," Susanna encouraged Phoebe.

"Oh, *Mamm,* look!" Phoebe said as she placed the little yellow booties near *Mamm* on the table. "Oh, Susanna, they're precious. *Denke!*"

"I made them," Susanna added shyly.

"They're my first baby thing so far. I will treasure them, for sure. Thank you!" Phoebe said, hugging Susanna and then leaving the little booties by *Mamm* who was examining one of them. Then Phoebe ushered her guests back out the door.

"This is Alice," Phoebe explained as they followed her into the barn. "Here, you hold these, and I'll hitch her up," Phoebe said as she showed Levi how to help.

"Let's go to the schoolhouse and then we can *kumm* back around and see the farm store. Miller's Mercantile has everything, and it's Amish-owned and run. After that, then the furniture barn where Stephen works. Oh, I can't believe you came to visit. This is so great," Phoebe said as she gave the reins a little shake.

Teacher Esther was busy grading papers when they arrived at the schoolhouse.

"Well, this is the school I went to and that my *mamm* went to, too, and our *kinner* will go to. It's seen a lot of families *kumm* through here. I taught here for three years, though that seems like a lifetime ago now," Phoebe reminisced.

"I took over when Phoebe went to college over a year ago now," Esther continued. "They're bringing the cords of wood over today for the winter, so we'll be all set. The building needs new insulation which they had hoped to put in this fall. We'll see," she said, rolling her eyes slightly.

They visited a bit and then returned to the buggy and made their way to Miller's Mercantile.

"We didn't get this far last time you were here, did we, Susanna?" Phoebe inquired.

"No. This looks interesting," she said as she hopped down from the buggy. They went in after Phoebe tied Alice up at the hitching rail. "They've got everything here you could ever need," Phoebe said.

"Quilts on this side, hardware over there, cloth, notions, canning jars, lamps, chimneys, wicks, even leather fan belts for your treadle sewing machine, toys," Phoebe listed the items up and down the aisles.

"I can't say I am unhappy I don't have a treadle sewing machine," Susanna laughed. "I'll take my Pfaff any day."

"Yours scares me. It almost ran over my fingers when I had a go at it when we visited. It runs like a race car and you can't stop it!" Phoebe said, shivering as she remembered the close call.

Levi wandered over to the fishing and tackle aisle of the store while the girls looked around the housewares department.

"They sure do have everything," Susanna marveled.

"Well, dearies, let's keep going, *ya?* We promised *Mamm* we'd help her out making dinner," Phoebe reminded them.

Back in the buggy, they headed out to see Stephen at the furniture barn.

"You're sure quiet, Mister," Susanna teased Levi.

"It's just so different. Like out of the olden days, but then it's not either," Levi observed. "I just didn't know what it would be like. Everything slows down, I guess. We end up running around all day, jump in the van to pick up one item at the hardware store, rush back, going all the time. But here it takes longer just to go somewhere. You get more time in the day though to work at home. Just interesting..." he trailed off.

They were soon at the furniture barn where Stephen had a thriving business going.

"Hi, I'm Stephen and this is my apprentice, Josiah," he began. "We only opened up in August and we already have orders lined up. Today we're working on kitchen cupboards for an older house that an Amish family just bought. We've ripped out the old ones and we'll get these in by next week. Knotty pine. We'll varnish them. They want them unstained and we'll put them up after they dry this weekend."

Phoebe introduced Levi and Susanna to Stephen.

"I wouldn't mind learning how to do cabinetry," Jacob noted. "You're lucky, Josiah, to have a master to teach you. We have a small carpentry shop, but nothing on this scale. It's something," he said. "Do you have electricity in here?" Jacob added.

"No, the equipment runs on compressed air. You wouldn't know the difference holding one of the tools. I learned without electricity, so I'm *gut* for now. I guess you don't miss what you haven't had," Stephen replied.

Phoebe suggested, then, "Why don't we leave Levi here with you and we'll go help *Mamm* with dinner?"

"*Gut* idea," Stephen agreed. Levi nodded his head, smiling. "Yup. I'd like that."

"See you all for dinner, then," Phoebe confirmed.

The girls made their way back to the house, unhitched Alice and led her to the paddock. *Mamm* was busy, happily humming when the girls came into the kitchen.

"Tell us what to do," Phoebe offered.

"Okay," *Mamm* thought a minute. "You two run down to the cellar and get up two jars of apple pie filling and Susanna, after you've seen the root cellar, maybe wash up and you can roll out those balls of dough on the side there, two tops and two straight in the pans."

The girls descended the stairs, holding a flashlight to see their way.

"*Mamm* is happiest when she'd giving orders," Phoebe chuckled.

"Look at all this!" Susanna exclaimed, wondering at the rows of jars. "You've been busy."

"No, this year it was all *Mamm's* doing. I was too busy for most of it with homework," Phoebe explained, grabbing the two jars and heading back upstairs.

"What are you making?" Phoebe inquired.

"The *roasht* is in the oven and I'm working on the gravy. Oh, that's like chicken and stuffing all mixed up together. We like that a lot," *Mamm* informed Susanna.

"I'll set the table, *Mamm*," Phoebe offered, "and get the water and the tea and coffee."

"*Gut*," *Mamm* agreed. "You can get the *bickel*—pickles, apple-sauce and beets out of the cooler and check on the green bean casserole for me. Just golden brown, not burnt. When that *kumms* out, you can stick in the pies."

"*Mamm*, I got you a present when I was at Miller's today. Close your eyes," Phoebe instructed from the sideboard. Her mother obediently closed her eyes as she wiped her hands off on her black apron.

"Okay, put out your hands," she teased.

When *Mamm* had done that, Phoebe placed a small brown bag into her hands.

"What is it?" *Mamm* puzzled.

"It's a pound of hazelnut decaffeinated coffee and a box of monk fruit sweetener. You are all set now," Phoebe encouraged her.

"Pffft," *Mamm* sputtered as she set the bag on the table, turning back to the stove.

"I'll make you a mug, you'll see. It's like stopping at Starbucks when we go to town," Phoebe said as she set the bag back on the sideboard and measured coffee into the French press she had been gifted with at her bridal shower. She carefully moved past *Mamm* at the stove and retrieved the tea kettle from the back burner. "We just wait five minutes now," she instructed. When it was ready, she took the spoon from *Mamm* and encouraged her to sit down. "I'll finish the gravy," she insisted. "It's ready. I already added the cream, *Mamm*."

Wiping her hands on her black apron once again and smoothing back the hairs sticking to her forehead, carefully tucking them under her *kapp, Mamm* sat back and lifted the mug to her lips, still scowling. She took a second sip and looked at Phoebe, her eyebrows raised.

"That really is like Starbucks," she said, shocked. "It's very *gut*. Special, even."

"I told you!" Phoebe laughed. "And it's *gut* for you!"

"*Ya*, I could get used to this. *Denke,* Phoebe. I like it," she answered, surprising even herself. Just then, the grandfather clock in the living room struck one o'clock.

"They'll be here any minute," *Mamm* said, jumping up. "You get the gravy boat out and put everything on the table," *Mamm* said, quickly back in action.

"I'll check the pies," Susanna offered. Then looking into the oven she said, "They'll take another ten minutes I think," she said, grabbing the kitchen timer from the top shelf of the warming oven and setting it to ten.

Soon everyone was seated around the table and enjoying the *Amische roasht*.

"This is amazing," Susanna declared. "How do you make it?"

"Remind me to give you the recipe after dinner," Phoebe promised. "It's basically stuffing, but on the outside with the chicken or turkey chopped up and put into it."

"Whoever thought up these things?" Susanna wondered. "Maybe some mom with a bunch of leftover stuffing and bits of chicken. Who knows? It's absolutely delicious."

"Mm-mmm," was all Levi could say in agreement with his mouth full.

Then Stephen spoke. "I've offered to take Levi on as an apprentice when Josiah goes back to Ohio. His community will give him a car for the duration and I get a helper out of it."

"I've always wanted to learn carpentry. I work sometimes in our shop, but the work Stephen is doing is quite different on a whole 'nother scale. I could bring some new ideas home," Levi said. "I'd never get a chance like this in the Hutterite colonies. At home, they think it's a great chance. I called my dad already," he said, pulling his cell phone out of his pocket.

Phoebe excused herself to put the coffee on and take the pies out of the oven. She carefully poured the last cup of *Mamm's* decaffeinated coffee from the French press through a strainer and into a small saucepan to warm on the stove.

"I won't be needin' dessert," *Mamm* said to Phoebe, smiling. "That coffee is enough of a special dessert by itself. I never knew it could be this *gut.*"

Just then, Phoebe had an idea. "Why don't you two stay for the *youngie* singing this evening? Do you mind driving home at night? Levi might enjoy seeing that."

"Oh, Levi, you've got to. I told you all about it, remember?" Susanna said excitedly.

"*Yo,*" Jacob began slowly. "I might just meet someone there, *ya* never know...."

Susanna promptly slapped his shoulder. "You will not!"

"Okay, let's go. Will you and Stephen come too?" Susanna asked.

"Sure," Stephen answered. "We don't need to leave till five," he said, looking to Phoebe.

"Oh, that will be fun. Let's," Phoebe agreed.

Then Levi added, "Let's go in our van, if it's okay with you, and then we can drop you off here and drive home after and it won't be all that late." Levi had already calculated that it would take hours later if they took the horse and buggy.

"Perfect," Stephen said. Then Susanna suggested, "Why don't we clean up and let your mom relax a bit? She's done enough, making this fabulous meal for us."

"That's decided then," Phoebe concurred.

"Any more of that *gut* coffee left?" *Mamm* asked.

"Kumming right up," Phoebe said.

"Since we've got all this manpower, I'm wondering if we shouldn't tackle that fence by the paddock this afternoon. It won't take us long," *Dat* suggested. The young men nodded, stretching as they got up to head out, more ready for a nap than work, but more than willing to help out.

"See you all later," Phoebe called as she poured *Mamm's* coffee.

Chapter Twenty-Four

Ben had hired a driver for the next Saturday so he could spend time with Leah and her family over the weekend. It was his last weekend visit. He was moving later that week to begin his life as a Mennonite. The Brennemans, friends of Leah's family, had graciously offered their spare room to Ben for as long as he needed it.

Leah had warned him that their entire church community was anxious to get to know Ben and welcome him into the fold. They weren't as eager as some sects to gain members, simply for the sake of quantity—numbers of members or boasting rights—but were genuinely interested in this young man who was braving all to marry his sweetheart. She hesitantly told him that they would be inundated with invitations to dinners, suppers, breakfasts even, from families vying to have him over to their houses and that he'd better have a small notebook and pencil to write it all down so he doesn't get mixed up because it would look like he stood people up.

His reply was, "I don't have any pockets, so I am appointing you my secretary, and you can keep track of our schedule, eh?"

The driver took the exit off the main road and entered into what Leah's father called 'Mennonite Territory.' As soon as they were on their way after the exit, sure enough, the signs once again appeared, exhorting any who read them to reform their lives if they hadn't already. Ben pointed the first one out to the driver.

"See, there's one," he explained. It read in big bold letters above the mailbox, YOU MUST BE BORN AGAIN... READ JOHN 3.

Then the driver perked up. "There's another one," he said, reading it aloud, BOUND BY SIN? JESUS CHRIST BRINGS FREEDOM!... READ JOHN 8. Then he added, "These people sound serious," he stated.

"Oh, they're the real deal," Ben assured him. "Look, there's one," he said, pointing off to the left. It read, JESUS CLAIMS TROUBLED HEARTS... READ JOHN 14.

Finally, the GPS in the car brought them to Leah's home. Leah, her mom, and the children had been waiting for him. Leah's father was working a half day at the lumber mill.

Ben was warmly welcomed and joined the family in the kitchen around the table.

"We just finished baking cookies. Coffee?" Leah's mother offered.

"*Ya*, thank you," Ben said, fully relaxing into the chair. "It's almost like I've known you all my whole life. It feels like home here."

"It *is* your home now," Leah's mother gently offered.

"Who would have thought five years ago that I would be here?" he mused.

"We are so grateful how God has led you, Ben," she answered.

"He has, every step of the way. I thank Him every day," he said, turning toward Leah and taking her hand under the table.

"I made the Cwunchy Cwisps," Simon informed Ben.

"And I made the *Pfeffernusse*," Yacob announced.

"So who made the molasses crinkles, then?" Ben teased.

"I did," Yofef answered, shyly.

"Wow, you could all become professional bakers by the time you're my age," Ben told them.

"No, I want to be a fireman," Yacob told Ben.

Taking his cue from his older brother, Simon said, "I want to be a firetruck," to which they all laughed.

"You can't be a fire truck," Leah corrected him. "You're a *person.*"

At that, Simon sat still, puzzling over the revelation.

"I'm going to work with Dad at the mill," Yosef declared.

"What are you gonna be when you grow up?" Simon asked Ben, at which everyone laughed again.

"Well, I dunno," Ben teased. "Maybe work with your dad, too. Would that be *gut?*"

"Why does he talk funny?" Simon asked, turning toward his mom.

"I'll answer that one," Ben jumped in. "I *kumm* from an Amish settlement. You knew that, right?" The boys all nodded their heads.

"Well, at home we speak Pennsylvania Dutch. It's sort a mix of languages from Germany, Switzerland, Austria and the Netherlands where my people came to America and Canada from originally. Your sister is actually trying to learn it. Did she tell you? Then we can talk together and you *kinner* won't have a clue what we're saying," Ben said, teasing them again.

"And neither will we," Leah's mother added, chuckling. "So you only learned English in school?" she asked Ben.

"That's right. Until I was six, I didn't know any English," Ben explained. "So, I guess I do talk funny. I use the *Deitsch* word for things if I can't think of the English words quick enough. So, *kaanscht du muukka funge? Ich kaanscht won sie hucke believe, aver sie bleib net.*"

The boys and their mother sat dumbfounded, Simon's mouth still open.

"He said, 'can you catch flies? I can if they remain sitting but they don't stay,'" Leah answered for Ben.

"Did you understand all that, Leah?" her mother asked, marveling that Leah might have actually become that proficient in such a short amount of time.

"No way," she answered, laughing. "It's sort of a joke between us. Someday maybe I'll speak that well."

"Are you gonna learn to drive a car or are you bringing your horse and buggy with you?" the oldest boy asked Ben.

"Maybe I could later. Would you like that?" Ben asked. The three little boys all bobbed their heads yes with their mouths full of cookies.

They finished their snack and then Ben followed the boys

around and pitched in as they did their chores. The first stop in the barn was where he was introduced to the pigs.

The pigs ran up to the gate of their stall, snorting and jostling each other while hoping for a tasty handout or a friendly scratch on the nose. Two of the boys had picked up an apple each off the ground as they left the house, knowing how their pigs loved them.

"This one is called Bacon," Yosef announced, holding out a wormy apple, which the pig lapped up in the blink of an eye.

"And this is Scrapple," Yacob told Ben. That pig also instantly snarfed up the proffered delicacy.

Simon explained, "Mom says they aren't pets, so we can't get attached to them," as he scratched the giant animal on its forehead. Then quoting his parents verbatim, he repeated, "Pigs are for food and always get butchered in the fall."

There were eggs to collect, fresh straw to lay in the hen house after it was first mucked out, the garden to hand harrow with the disc implement, rose bushes to wrap in burlap for the winter and plenty of other jobs their father had assigned to them at breakfast earlier that day. The yard still had a few plantain weeds to ferret out with the dandelion weeder, the job usually reserved for punishment when one of the boys went astray, like the last time Yosef put salt in the sugar bowl and sugar in the saltshaker. His friend at school had clued him in to the little prank. Hosea had failed to inform Yosef that the consequences for his little prank had earned him the task of scrubbing out the outhouse by the barn with Lysol —walls, steps, ceiling and all.

If they got all that done, they were to see if there were any wild African violets or ground cherries or rose hips left in the field for their mom to make jellies with.

Leah stayed behind with her mother to help around the house.

"What should we make for dinner?" her mom asked after the laundry had all been put away.

"I don't know. Do you have any ideas?" Leah asked.

"I know," her mom perked up. "Corn fritters and stuffed green peppers."

"Oh, yum. Yes," Leah agreed. "I could make a dessert then."

The menu agreed upon, both women went to work.

"I thawed out the hamburger last night, so this won't take long," her mom said while Leah paged through the cookbook.

"How 'bout a gingerbread cake with hot lemon sauce?" Leah said, stopping at the page.

"Yes, that sounds good. I get the feeling Ben will enjoy anything you make," her mother said.

"I know. He's not fussy at all. So down-to-earth. That's what I love about him, Mom. I still can't believe we found each other. And he is so generous, all the time, and optimistic, in spite of everything. Isn't it a mystery?" she asked. "He makes me think of your 'Rules' framed over there on the wall." Leah proceeded to read the "Rules" aloud,

Rules for Doing Good.

Do all the good you can,
In all the ways you can,
To all the People you can,
At all the times you can,
As long as ever you can.

"He is quite a young man. I will be proud to call him my son-in-law," Leah's mom said, blinking back tears. "We better get a move-on here, now. Dinner won't make itself," she reminded Leah.

Chapter Twenty-Five

Phoebe was taking advantage of a rare, quiet Saturday afternoon. Stephen had gone into the next town right after dinner to pick up some hardware items for a job he was working on. *Dat* was in the barn hoping to finish earlier today and be able to relax a bit with *The Budget* before supper. *Mamm* was taking a nap, a luxury she greedily indulged in when the house appeared to be presentable, should uninvited guests show up. Without having a telephone and relying on snail mail from friends and family informing one of planned or impending visits, if you are Amish at least, you need to keep the house in decent form at all times so as not to be embarrassed by a mess should someone turn up completely unexpected.

Her homework was actually caught up today. The reading could wait until Sunday afternoon since it didn't appear to be a huge amount. Phoebe hunted through the boxes in the top of the closet in the hallway, where she stored all sorts of things too precious to give away but not needed just now, if ever. Like her old calligraphy set and watercolors. Her pencil case of brushes was in the box, too, as was her collection of books on embroidery and quilting. But today she was after the calligraphy set. *Good, there is still ink in the bottle,* she noted to herself, *and plenty of fine card stock, too.*

Phoebe had woken up thinking of the set of rules she had carefully written out for her classroom at the beginning of her first term as a teacher. It would be perfect to hang in the house as their little ones grew up. She brought the items to the little drop-wing table in the *dawdi haus* they were living in until she finished school and spread everything out to begin. Carefully drawing barely visible pencil lines and measuring the spaces between them with a ruler, she mapped out the list she would slowly pen there. It could be later mounted onto a wood plaque. Surely Stephen would know how to laminate it, finishing the job by putting a little picture hanger on the back. Pushing the marked page across the table, away from her workspace, she took out a regular piece of paper from her homework spiral and began practicing the alphabet, knowing she would be rusty from not having written in calligraphy in such a long time.

Has it already been two years since I taught school? Almost three it must be by now. And to think of all that has happened since then, she pondered. *Stephen, for one. I didn't see that* kumming *for sure. I was certain I'd be an old* maud.... *There is such joy in loving someone, sharing that love. I had no clue about that either. And I didn't have to marry some old widower, but then, I 'spose someone has to marry them. I am just glad* Gott *didn't want me to do that, actually. Or He could have sent me a cow farmer, but I guess I would swallow that too, if I had to, if I'd already fallen in love. And having a* bobbeli *now besides. Not in my wildest dreams. What else have You got in store for us, eh? If only we would all trust more, have perfect faith in You. Then no one would get depressed or despair; there wouldn't be so much suffering in the world. You have for sure not made this life easy, but I guess that is part of the plan, eh? I just wonder sometimes. But then every life has difficulties, problems, stress, and tensions. We can't escape that. Is that all just part of life on earth then? And then Jesus comes to fill in the gaps with pure joy. He makes life worth living, even among all the suffering. Then we have a purpose, and that leads to happiness, which He promises to carry with us. Well, it's all too great for me. I'll never understand it all. I still wonder though....*

An hour later, satisfied that she was remembering how to do it correctly, she began drawing an embellished R at the top of the good card stock. *So far, so* gut, she thought to herself. *Stephen won't be home till supper time, and* Mamm *and I can put that together rather quickly, so I'll be able to make a start today. Some of these sayings don't exactly fit outside the classroom, but I like how it's been hanging in Amish schoolhouses all these decades, getting close to a hundred years, since 1930 was the first Amish schoolhouse in Lancaster, Pennsylvania.*

After another hour passed while Phoebe was ever so slowly writing out each line. She stood up to stretch and make herself a cup of tea. Carefully setting the mug down on the table, she resumed her meticulous task. By four p.m. it was finished.

Rules
Come in and sit down immediately.
Do not use bad or unclean language.
Help along with the singing.
Do not play on the outhouse roof during recess.
Be humble and do not openly correct the teacher of any mistakes.
Do not write on books or school property.
Do not leave the school grounds without permission.
Be thankful, honest and respectful at all times.

When Stephen came home, along with Josiah, his apprentice, *Mamm* and Phoebe had supper ready and waiting on the table. The Yankee bean soup was still bubbling on the stove, sweetened with molasses and spiced with salt pork. Fresh corn bread, already cut into hefty slabs, new butter, and maple syrup—one of the last of twelve bottles left until more sap started running should they see a thaw as early as sometime in February—were already set out. A bowl of canned Georgia peaches sat in their glossy syrup further down the table, next to a bowl of dill pickles. The lamps were lit and the good aromas met all those coming in from outside. *Dat* was still dozing in his hickory and oak bent wood rocking chair with *The Budget* open on his lap. The ads pages had already slithered their way down to the floor by his stockinged feet.

All the bustle of everyone coming in and hanging up coats and hats and kicking off barn boots was enough to waken the old man. He quickly lifted the paper, pushing his glasses further up his nose and continued reading where he'd left off. Then, addressing whoever might want to hear, he read out loud, first commenting on the text,

"Maudie has out-done herself this time. Whoever thinks up these things? What's wrong with plain old farm cooking? All these new-fangled ideas. Maybe she's just running out of ideas and getting desperate. Listen to this one: 'Ranch Pizza'" he began. "After you make the pizza dough—she tells you how to do that all of course—then you mix half a cup of mayonnaise with half a cup of ranch dressing and spoon it onto the dough instead of tomato sauce. Then you pile on peppers, onions, mushrooms, olives, chunks of cooked chicken, ground beef or ham and all the cheese on top of that. Bake at 400 degrees for twenty minutes. *Mamm,* can you hear me? Don't get any ideas, please."

Mamm walked over to *Dat* and demurely answered him, "No dear, I won't be making Ranch Pizza. I promise. Now *kumm* to the table," she said, bending over and picking up the ads scattered on the floor.

"I have a surprise for you after supper," Phoebe whispered to Stephen after he sat down. She slid into her seat and folded her hands in her lap. After the silent grace, she jumped up and brought the soup pot to the table and served it up as everyone passed their bowls down to her.

"I can't wait," Stephen whispered back as she once again sat down next to him, taking her hand in his under the table and stroked it.

Chapter Twenty-Six

S usanna was visiting her *ankela* for the weekend. Her grandmother lived at another colony where her sons had settled with their families. *Ankela* could visit any one of them any time she wanted. Many Hutterian colonies housed multiple families with the same last name, often reflecting the founding families of each settlement. For example, the Deckers at one time populated Pembrook Colony almost exclusively. The Maendels are the majority of the members in certain colonies in Canada and the Tschetters are the majority in Tschetter Colony in Olivet, South Dakota. Other names include the Hofers, Waldners, Wurtzes, Kleinsassers, Glanzers, Stahls, Walthers, Wollmans, and Grosses, who make up the fourteen Hutterite surnames in existence today.

Ankela was ensconced in her reclining lounge chair in the living room of her eldest son, Tim's house when Susanna found her. Susanna quickly put on the electric coffee pot and rummaged through the snack cupboard until she found what she was looking for: two Mars bars, her grandmother's favorite snack.

Fixing two mugs, she brought the tray to the coffee table, which was sitting on a faux fur rug there. The living room was simple enough, but the attempt at style was also evident. A John Deere calendar hung next to the window. A wall clock hung above a handmade oak desk. The clock was mounted on a holographic picture of a deer pausing in a clearing in a woods. The clock had recently joined the list of innovative designs being made in carpentry shops among the colonies. A Rubrik's cube sat next to a cut glass candy dish filled with Jolly Ranchers on the coffee table. A puzzle sat next to the candy, a brainteaser made from bent horseshoe nails that interlocked. On the floor next to the lounge chair was a large basket holding the beginnings of a folded polyester squares rug. *Ankelas* in many of the colonies have taken up this older craft using worn clothing and cutting tiny one-inch squares out of the fabric. Then an oval rug-sized backing is sewn in a spiral fashion, usually on a heavy-duty or industrial machine, inserting the diagonally folded tiny bits one after another under the needle until the backing is covered with the tightly spaced bits. The finished product will last for years, is washable and never needs mending.

Ankela was busy crocheting what she called 'chair booties.' Each one was started by casting on twelve stitches with yarn and then crocheting in a circle until the finished item was about three inches tall, a little crocheted tube that was meant to fit over each of the four feet of the kitchen chairs to avoid skid marks on the kitchen's linoleum floors. Eight kitchen chairs would require a total of thirty-two little 'socks' or booties. If each of her six sons had eight kitchen chairs in their homes, she would have to make one hundred and ninety-two of them to accommodate them all.

She could also sell them at the roadside stand some of the young people ran all summer. There were plenty of crafts for sale there, along with canned pickles and jams and jellies and garden produce. She had her work cut out for her, though she was happy to have something to do during the long hours each day. During good weather, she could always sit outside in the courtyard of the dwelling houses or wander over to the *klanaschuel* and visit the babies there. There were always other *ankelas* who would welcome a visitor, or she could snoop around the communal kitchen and see what is on the menu that day, perhaps helping to roll out buns or help wrap cookies for the freezers.

Her daughters-in-law were often at home during the day, especially if they had young children. They had plenty to do mending clothes and sewing new items for their ever-growing brood. She could always help there, darning a sock or sewing on buttons or snaps, though the bright pearl-colored hammered-in snaps were quickly becoming all the rage in most colonies these days.

A harmonica could be heard down the hall, the musician obviously new to the instrument, as Susanna settled on the hand-upholstered regulation sofa. Actually, the sofa was handmade from the same pattern that had been used for decades in numerous colonies. There was no need to change something that already worked just fine. The *Ordnung* didn't dictate furniture patterns, but tradition has appeared to have become frozen in time in the observance of ongoing Hutterite life.

"I've got a good one for you, *Ankela*," Susanna began. "I've told you I am in nursing school with an Amish girl and two Mennonites, *ya?*"

Ankela nodded, taking a tentative sip of the steaming coffee.

Susanna went on. "Well, at lunch time this week when we all met up, Hilde told me that the bishop's wife had phoned and asked if she could come over sometime because she had some medical questions for her. So she went there the other evening after school and she followed the *basel* into the bedroom so they could talk in private. Well, she sat on the chair there and indicated that Hilde sit on the end of the bed, but when she went to sit down, she literally *fell* into it. The Mennonite bishop has a waterbed of all things! The woman explained to Hilde that their chiropractor had recommended it to help with his arthritic knees and hips. Can you believe it?" Susanna broke out laughing.

"*Yo,* that's a good one," *Ankela* agreed.

"They have electricity like we do, so heating it in the winter isn't a problem. I doubt we'll find a waterbed in an Amish home, though," Susanna added, still rocking with laughter.

"So, the wedding is coming up soon?" *Ankela* asked.

"I can't wait. It's so exciting. Did I tell you Levi will be studying carpentry under an Amish fellow? He'll come back every evening. He is so charged up about it. Maybe we'll end up with a fancy cupboard or something. I wouldn't mind a chiming clock, one with a glass door instead of one of these new moving pictures where the deer's eyes follow you around the room all day, you know the ones

Jake is cranking out here? Ugh. I won't miss those," Susanna shuddered at the thought.

Ankela laughed and reaching into her knitting basket, pulled out a package wrapped in tissue paper and handed it to Susanna, saying simply, "for you."

Susanna slowly opened it. "Oh, *Ankela!* This one was yours when I was growing up. Are you sure you want to give it away?"

"*Yo*, sure. It was made for us when we got married. It's sixty-five years old now. *Ol' Vetter* would want you two to have it."

Susanna carefully laid out the leather strip with ten small beveled decorative wooden plaques spaced out along it, with different words hand lettered onto each one beginning with "The Fruit of the Spirit is…" and each consecutive one reading those attributes from Galacians 5:22.

The Fruit of the Spirit is…
Love
Peace
Patience
Kindness
Generosity
Faithfulness
Gentleness
Self-control…Galacians 5:22

"Oh, I will always treasure this. Thank you! And I can give it to one of our grandchildren when they marry. I wish *Ol' Vetter* could have come to our wedding. You must miss him. It's only two years ago now, isn't it?" Susanna asked.

Ankela nodded and took another bite of her Mars bar.

Chapter Twenty-Seven

L eah and Ben were enjoying a rare drive in the countryside that Saturday morning, the only time she could afford to get away from her studies. She had learned to drive the summer before. Sunday would be filled with church and Ben's baptism instructions in the afternoon at the minister's house. Supper there would follow. Also attending would be the other four young people preparing for baptism. Ben would be the only one in the group not raised in the Mennonite tradition. He found the meetings interesting and exhilarating. The only difference he could find so far was in the interpretation of the gospels there as understood by each group, the Amish, or the Mennonites.

All of the Plain churches, which included the Hutterites, too, shared more that was the same or similar than there were differences. Only the fine points of each tradition in dogma or theology seemed to pose a stumbling block between them, but as far as Ben was concerned should never have separated them from the beginning. Quibbling over the level of engagement in 'the world' seemed a poor excuse to keep Christians apart all these centuries. Why couldn't they all agree to disagree, for goodness' sakes? But history, cultures, wars, persecution and pigheadedness seemed to have wrought the divisions, at least as far as Ben could figure.

He continued to see no obstacle to being able to agree with the faith he was bound and determined to embrace for the rest of his life for the sake of his bride-to-be.

"I have a surprise for you," Ben announced as they passed yet another Mennonite mailbox sign on the road. This one read PEACE IS KNOWING JESUS... READ JOHN 14:27.

"What is it?" Leah begged, keeping her eyes on the road. Ben turned and reached into a canvas bag to remove his wallet. Opening it, he found what he wanted to show her. Holding it up, he held his new driver's permit announcing, "I got it on Wednesday. Can I have a turn next?" he asked, grinning from ear to ear.

"Oh! That's great, Ben. Yes. Let's start off at the parking lot in town, okay? We can't get into too much trouble there."

"Actually, I never told you. During my *rumschpringe* years, my buddy Moses had a car and let me drive it a bit. I didn't have a proper license, could have gotten arrested for some of our *mufti*, but I was lucky,"

"More like your guardian angel had a run for his money, I'd say," Leah stated.

"*Ya*, but I survived my rite of passage jumping around and all, getting into enough trouble. One time, Moses and me were in town, with his car, we couldn't have been seventeen yet, and we went to the general store and decided to try shoplifting. It was on a dare. We each grabbed a fistful of BB shot and just as we thought we'd gotten away with it we see the clerk heading down our aisle and we both decided at the same time to throw the stuff into our mouths and swallow them to destroy the evidence.

Well, the guy saw us though he didn't know what we'd swallowed—could have been sunflower seeds or something for all he knew—so he couldn't do anything. We hightailed it outta there. Later that night, after supper, we hear a buggy crunching on the gravel on our drive. It's Moses' *dat* who told my *dat* that Moses had gotten sick that afternoon, and finally confessed what we'd done and they took him to the hospital where they x-rayed his stomach and decided to pump them all outta him. So I got dragged in, too. That for sure cured me of ever shoplifting again. Ugh."

"Yep, that would do it," Leah replied, laughing. "Kids can be pretty dumb. Stupid, I'd say. Maybe they're supposed to be stupid, part of being a kid. Did I tell you about the time I stuck something up my nose to see how far it would go?" Ben shook his head no and laughed.

"Do I really wanna hear this?" he hesitated.

"Well, it was up there pretty good," she continued, "and after a few days my mom thought I had a cold cause I kept sniffling, and then she thought I had the flu or something.

"One day she was changing my diaper. I was only two, and while I was lying on my back, she could see up my nose and called Dad. She thought it looked funny, like white when it should look pink. So they called the doctor and asked if they should bring me into the emergency room. He thought a minute about it and said, 'Well, there's something up there that shouldn't be...and the only difference between my tweezers at the hospital and yours at home is about $300, so why don't I stay on the line and talk you through this? Put her up on a counter and wrap her arms in a towel or something and just have her dad hold her head still like that. Then see if you can pull it out. It's okay if you scratch her nose a bit, you might see a little blood, but that's okay. Let me know... I'll stay on the line.'

"While they were doing that I kept screaming, 'you're 'queezing me! You're 'queezing me!' So they did that and pulled a big hunk of foam rubber out. They looked again, and it was still white inside, so Mom tried it again and got another hunk of foam out. That was it. They untied me then, and I sat up and sniffed a few times, finally able to breathe properly and happy to be let loose. They told the doctor she seemed good, who pronounced Mom a decent surgeon. Later they found a tiny hole in the sofa where I'd been pulling out bits of stuffing." By this time Leah and Ben were both laughing so hard they had to wipe their eyes.

They spent the afternoon in the Kmart parking lot in the next town, driving around in circles and backing into a spot, and then driving around the other way and parallel parking.

"I pronounce you ready to take your driving test. You're doing just fine, Mister," Leah declared. "Let's head home. Want to drive?" she asked.

"Sure," he said, but hesitated. Then Ben brought up the subject he had been mulling over since he'd moved to the Mennonite community. It had kept him up nights, trying to wrap his head around this one. Should he? Shouldn't he? Was it too soon? Was it what was expected of him? What would it feel like? In the final analysis, he decided it was probably the most minor parts of his conversion, but it felt like going against everything he was brought up thinking. Should feeling guilt or shame be part of the equation? He didn't believe so. Did it *really* matter to God in the greater scheme of all Eternity, what color his shirt was or how short his hair was cut? Was he actually blindly conforming to a culture or was he sincerely seeking to find the way God had called him to? And would the questions in his mind ever end?

"Well, Leah, I am wondering about picking up some jeans and shirts while we're here. What do you think?"

"Why?" she asked, completely confused by this unexpected turn in their conversation.

"Do you mean for you?"

"*Ya.* Like is it too soon, or is your family expecting me to? I'm not sure what to do," he answered honestly.

"Well, we don't have rules about that. It's up to you, really. It isn't that big a deal, I don't think," she guessed. "We could ask my dad...."

"I think it's just up to me if I am ready. *Kumm.* We're going shopping at Kmart since we're here," he said, taking the keys out of the ignition.

A few heads turned as they made their way down the men's wear aisle, holding hands no less. This unlikely pair, though most English people wouldn't know the difference at a glance that one was Amish and the other Mennonite. Most thought they all looked the same in reality.

It took about two hours to find jeans that weren't skin-tight, which was all the rage just then, and shirts that didn't have cowboy motifs on them. Finally satisfied with his purchases, they headed for the store's exit.

"Wait," Ben said. "I think I'll change here and surprise your family when we get back."

"You're ready?" Leah asked.

"Heck, yes. Ready as I'll ever be, I guess," he said, making an about face and heading off to find the men's room.

Leah waited for Ben in the aisle outside the rest rooms. When Ben finally appeared, blushing like a schoolgirl, his Amish clothes stuffed into a shopping bag, Leah started laughing, covering her mouth with her free hand.

"Does it look okay?" Ben asked. "Do I look silly?"

"It's fine. You just look cute. I didn't know how you'd be looking regular, you know, not Amish," she chuckled.

"So, will you keep me?" he teased.

"Absolutely, honey," she giggled, taking his hand and heading for the car.

"Now I just need a haircut. Anything still open, *ya* think?" Ben asked.

"Oh! You're really ready? Maybe you should just get used to the clothes first?" Leah asked.

"I dunno. Why not?" Ben replied. "I'm sure," he said, grinning from ear to ear. He leaned over the seat and pulled Leah toward himself, kissing her on the cheek.

"I've never been so happy. I love you, Leah."

"And I've never been so in love. You are so special, Ben. I can't believe we are really getting married. Can you? God is so good."

Chapter Twenty-Eight

Finally, they were back, heading out to the county road.

"It will take me awhile to get used to the new you," Leah said, reaching out to ruffle his short hair, still chuckling as Ben drove.

"Your poor *Mamm*. Do you think she'll understand? Wanting to fit in, to move forward, and not doing it to renounce your past?" Leah asked.

"We grow up exactly where *Gott* wants us. It's all part of His plan. I've committed my life to what I believe *because* of how I was raised. I wish she could see that," Ben explained with a sigh.

Soon they were back in Mennonite Territory, as Leah's dad called it, evidenced by the signs appearing once again. The first one said, WHERE WILL YOU SPEND ETERNITY? ... READ HEBREWS 9: 27.

"I kind of like the signs, *ya* know," Ben said. "They just remind you to keep your thoughts turned to what's important. Have you ever gotten any backlash with them?"

"The only thing is that every so often some kids joy riding at night might get handy with the spray paint, but it doesn't happen too often. Only once last year if I remember right," Leah recalled.

"Our bake sale took a hit a few years ago," Ben began. "Our neighbor, Enoch, noticed something funny about the bake sale sign he had just passed on the road on his way to the Gingerich's farm with his wife Suzy's funnel cakes she had made the day before. Enoch stopped and backed up the horse and buggy so he could take another look. The sign looked like it had been spray-painted over the white lettering on the blackboard. He saw more desecrated signs as he neared the farm where the bake sale had been set up. There were even red spray-painted swastikas on some of the signs."

"As he pulled into the farm, he saw some of the men gathered by the barn talking quite earnestly. He tied his horse to the hitching post and joined them. They had seen the signs too. They were discussing what they should do about it. Actually, there was nothing they could do: we *Amische* profess pacifism. We won't go to court to sue anyone, no matter how wrong they be; we won't enlist or carry weapons either. Someone had made it clear they didn't want their *Amische* neighbors having a bake sale that day. The answer was simple. It has been decided. Everyone take your pies and go home."

"Then one of their *Englische* neighbors arrived after most of the folks had already gone and the few left were packing up their baked goods and hitching up their buggies. The way Esme Gingerich recalls it, the neighbor went directly to the back door and found her and said, 'You can't be serious! You'd cancel the whole thing because of a few teenagers? I am sure it was just a stupid prank,' So Esme replies 'They don't want it, and we don't argue with them.' And the neighbor goes on, 'but it's just plain vandalism, just some kids with nothing better to do than fool around with a paint can,' so Esme straightens up and looks sternly at her and says, 'It isn't wanted. THAT... IS... IT,' and so she quietly closed the conversation."

"Wow," Leah replied.

"Yeah. We ate cake and pie for every meal for a week after that. *Mamm* had to bring home all that baked stuff she had made for it. Us kids didn't complain. *Dat* neither. We must have been holy terrors with all that sugar on board."

"My mom didn't even have sugar in the house till we were older. She tried using only honey for a while. We didn't have candy except when we went to *Oma's* house. That was a treat, then," Leah explained. "She even figured out how to do the canning without it. I guess she used honey instead somehow. She had this saying, 'eat what you can and can what you can't.' I thought that was clever."

"My *mamm* had one too: " 'Always have a well-stocked pantry, just in case things get bad.' Maybe that came one out of the Depression."

"Oh, there's another sign, look." Ben slowed the car as they passed the mailbox. He read, SEEK GOD WITH YOUR WHOLE HEART... READ MATTHEW 6:33, and then turned into the driveway. They were home.

Chapter Twenty-Nine

Supper was over and Phoebe and *Mamm* were still sitting at the table. The dishes were piled up in the sink while the hot water was heating on the stove. *Mamm* was enjoying a leisurely second cup of decaffeinated coffee while she carefully pushed the last crumbs of her pie onto the edge of the plate, licked her finger and picking them up, popped them into her mouth.

"Our baby is the size of a small lemon this week and will be the size of an apple next week," Phoebe randomly announced.

"I'll never get used to you calling your baby a lemon or an apple and all. It's almost, almost, *ach*, disrespectful, that's what it is," *Mamm* complained.

"I just like thinking how plump it's growing," Phoebe commented.

"Well, I'll never understand this next generation. All these *ferhoodled* ideas about... just about everything, babies and birth. I suppose you'll breastfeed, too?" *Mamm* challenged her.

"*Mamm,* you know what *Grossmammi* says about that? 'It's always warm, it's always ready, and it's up high where the cats can't get it!'" Phoebe laughed. *Mamm* had to chuckle along with her.

"Let's do up the dishes," Phoebe suggested.

"Okay," *Mamm* said. "And then it will probably be time for you and that little lemon of yours to go to bed," she added shaking her head though she was chuckling too. "Just so long as you don't name her Lemonade!"

"Maybe Apple Pie then?" Phoebe added.

The next day, Leah was waiting for Ben to arrive. She would use the time to review the next week's lessons until it was time to go to church together. She was wearing her new rose-colored calico dress. She'd just put the finishing touches on it last night. Her mother was sewing her wedding dress. It would be modest, but they were taking a few liberties with it. A slightly scooped neck and puffy three-quarter length sleeve were a small nod at style, and it was made out of white percale, with an embroidered white floral pattern throughout. She would carry flowers and still wear her small stiff white bonnet over her bun. With Ben's baptism scheduled for the last week in November, they could set a wedding date. They wouldn't wait until she graduated then. Sometime before the Christmas festivities got into full swing would be perfect. Even her parents approved.

She heard the car door slam and quickly closed the textbook. They had plenty of time before they had to leave. She'd offer him coffee and a sticky bun. They would ride with her family. There was plenty of room in the new big Dodge van.

Hilde would be at church today, too. Leah had wondered how she and Ivan were getting on. She'd make a point of asking her.

Hilde and Ivan were not in complete agreement it turned out. His family's visit from Indiana was over, and they were all packed and ready to return the next day. The couple had brainstormed together, trying to come up with a way that he could stay on, but he had taken time off of work for the trip and his boss was expecting him back on the construction crew early Monday morning. Hilde was afraid their relationship could cool off if they were apart for a time. He was just as worried that she would get caught up in some project after she graduated and not be as serious about the relationship as she seemed right now.

"I think we need to trust each other more," Ivan began. "We know God has brought us together, and if it was meant to be, then nothing will come between us. We'll need to pray for that trust and faith, and write letters a whole lot too," he said, smiling and squeezing her hands in his.

In truth, it had been a very short time since they first met, but they both felt different about this relationship. They weren't wearing rose-colored glasses by any means. Neither felt the need to date just for fun, as if they had time to get to know lots of folks and then had the luxury of choosing the best apple in the basket. Rather, hadn't they already put all of their faith in a Creator who also had the perfect helpmate already chosen for each one? Both wondered if they'd found 'the one' and after only three weeks, each felt that they were closer to their answer. But Hilde was also afraid that they could somehow sabotage God's plan if they didn't commit to each other somehow now. Could they miss this divine chance by their own neglect somehow? They knew their friendship was far more than superficial.

But then didn't she talk about going on a mission trip now that she was almost a nurse, and with her license she would be a valuable asset to any of the Mennonite teams in Africa or South America or Mexico, Ivan wondered. He was not a spring chicken anymore. How long was long enough to understand one's heart? What wasn't long enough? Where were the most important answers when you needed them? Independently, they each felt that they would only find their way through prayer. Ivan had been right. Hadn't he said they needed trust and prayer?

"I know. I can't believe it's been only three weeks. Maybe I could visit you over a long weekend, maybe over the holidays," she said, brightening up slightly.

"Yeah, let's plan on that," Ivan replied, and kissed her gently. Overcome with fear that he was leaving his beloved behind, he drew her to himself and engulfed her in a strong embrace. She wrapped her arms around his middle while she buried her head against his chest. Neither wanted to be the first to let go. Why couldn't they just remain like this forever? Well, reality, for one thing. There was work and school waiting for them on Monday. How could they possibly wait weeks or even months to be reunited? They couldn't imagine going forward without the other. Finally Ivan spoke.

"It won't be forever. It will be all that much sweeter next time I see you," he said.

"I'll miss you so much," she finally admitted.

Chapter Thirty

Stephen and Phoebe had just gotten back from seeing Roberta, their midwife. He had taken a couple of hours off, leaving the furniture barn in Levi's care right after lunch. There was more than enough to do that he could easily handle without Stephen looking over his shoulder every minute. Tools needed cleaning and oiling, the suction system needed emptying of all its sawdust, the floors could use a good sweep and a multitude of other tasks would keep him out of trouble.

Roberta had Phoebe lie down on the exam table and measured her stomach from top to bottom with a paper measuring tape. Then she felt her stomach, 'walking' her fingers around using her fingertips where she expected the baby to be settled snug inside her bag of waters. Then she took the paper measuring tape once again and measured Phoebe's stomach from side to side this time. Neither Stephen nor Phoebe noticed Roberta's puzzled look quite yet.

"Hang in there while I go get the Doppler," Roberta said as she left the exam room. She returned shortly and squirted the conducting gel onto the machine's wand before running it slowly across the expanding tummy. The instrument crackled for a bit until she came to the spot she was looking for and came to rest there. They could all hear the slow faint, blub, blub, blub sound then.

"That's your heartbeat," Roberta explained to the couple. Moving the wand further down, they could instantly hear a much faster, blub, blub sound.

"And that's your baby," she explained.

"It sounds more like a pony, than a baby in there," Stephen laughed.

Then, moving the wand back up the mound of her belly, Roberta brought it to rest once again at another point. Immediately, the Doppler again picked up the fast blub, blub, blub sounds.

"And that is your other baby," Roberta said, trying to keep a straight face. No one spoke as the Doppler continued to amplify this heartbeat around the room.

Stephen looked at Phoebe, who looked at Roberta, and then back to Stephen. They continued to try to take in this new revelation but appeared unable to do so. Shock can do that to a person. They were both rendered speechless.

Suddenly, Phoebe burst into tears. Stephen took her hand in his. All he could say was, "Are you sure? You're really sure? *Really?*" Stephen begged Roberta.

"Yes, I am sure. Congratulations!" Roberta assured them, chuckling.

The End

Coming Spring 2023

Playing on the Outhouse Roof, The Amish Nurse Series, Book 3

———————

Don't miss out on your next favorite book!

Join the Satin Romance mailing list
www.satinromance.com/mail.html

Acknowledgments

I have given birth to a series of books full of true stories and memories gathered from a lifetime of amazing encounters with other cultures and diverse peoples. Firstly, I want to thank my sister, the real Phebe Schwartz—yes, spelled without an 'o'--for the amazing job she did editing all the books in the series. I also want to thank my very own personal research assistant and librarian, Rosalyn Hope for her hours of hunting down every last one of my endless requests.

I also owe a great debt to the mothers and babies I have had the privilege of serving as a midwife for so many years and all I learned from each one: Amish *mamms*, Hutterite *mueters*, Hmong *nias*, Vietnamese *mę*, Somali *hoyo*, Ethiopian *haada,* and Native American *mantle* and all the other brave women I have met. Many thanks go to my Canadian Hutterite *basel-*friend who advised me when it came to *Hutterische* language and culture.

Eternal thanks to my publisher, Nancy Schumacher and the entire team at Melange Books, for believing in my writing. May I gift you with my first-born son as a sign of my gratitude? (He's really cute!)

I also owe a great debt of gratitude to Patricia Morris (past president of MIPA, Minnesota Independent Publishers Association,) WOW (Women of Words,) and NLW/RWA (Northern Lights Writers/ Minnesota chapter of Romance Writers of America,) all author-friends who have so unselfishly shared their wisdom and experience of the writing and publishing world with me. Special thanks go to my dear friend and author, Phyllis Moore for her love, prayers, advice and support.

Also, I want to thank my most vocal critics, Alexsi Currier and his wife Anastasia for reading the drafts and keeping me on my toes throughout the long months of the Pandemic. Of course, I can't end without expressing my eternal gratitude to my dearest husband of 46 years, David, and my children, Abraham, Isaac, Ruth, Rachel, and Hannah for their undying love, encouragement and support no matter how crazy mother's latest creation appears to be.

THANK YOU FOR READING

Did you enjoy this book?

We invite you to leave a review at the website of your choice, such as Goodreads, Amazon, Barnes & Noble, etc.

DID YOU KNOW THAT LEAVING A REVIEW...

- Helps other readers find books they may enjoy.
- Gives you a chance to let your voice be heard.
- Gives authors recognition for their hard work.
- Doesn't have to be long. A sentence or two about why you liked the book will do.